Charles Dickens – Nobody's Story & Other Short Stories

Charles Dickens (1812-1870) is regarded by many readers and literary critics to be THE major English novelist of the Victorian Age. He is remembered today as the author of a series of weighty novels which have been translated into many languages and promoted to the rank of World Classics. The latter include, but are not limited to, *The Adventures of Oliver Twist*, *A Tale of Two Cities*, *David Copperfield*, *A Christmas Carol*, *Hard Times*, *Great Expectations* and *The Old Curiosity Shop*.

Here we bring you a selection of his quite remarkable short stories.

Contents

Nobody's Story

He lived on the bank of a mighty river, broad and deep, which was always silently rolling on to a vast undiscovered ocean. It had rolled on, ever since the world began. It had changed its course sometimes, and turned into new channels, leaving its old ways dry and barren; but it had ever been upon the flow, and ever was to flow until Time should be no more. Against its strong, unfathomable stream, nothing made head. No living creature, no flower, no leaf, no particle of animate or inanimate existence, ever strayed back from the undiscovered ocean. The tide of the river set resistlessly towards it; and the tide never stopped, any more than the earth stops in its circling round the sun.

He lived in a busy place, and he worked very hard to live. He had no hope of ever being rich enough to live a month without hard work, but he was quite content, GOD knows, to labour with a cheerful will. He was one of an immense family, all of whose sons and daughters gained their daily bread by daily work, prolonged from their rising up betimes until their lying down at night. Beyond this destiny he had no prospect, and he sought none.

There was over-much drumming, trumpeting, and speech-making, in the neighbourhood where he dwelt; but he had nothing to do with that. Such clash and uproar came from the Bigwig family, at the unaccountable proceedings of which race, he marvelled much. They set up the strangest statues, in iron, marble, bronze, and brass, before his door; and darkened his house with the legs and tails of uncouth images of horses. He wondered what it all meant, smiled in a rough good-humoured way he had, and kept at his hard work.

The Bigwig family (composed of all the stateliest people thereabouts, and all the noisiest) had undertaken to save him the trouble of thinking for himself, and to manage him and his affairs. "Why truly," said he, "I have little time upon my hands; and if you will be so good as to take care of me, in return for the money I pay over", for the Bigwig family were not above his money, "I shall be relieved and much obliged, considering that you know best." Hence the drumming, trumpeting, and speech-making, and the ugly images of horses which he was expected to fall down and worship.

"I don't understand all this," said he, rubbing his furrowed brow confusedly. "But it HAS a meaning, maybe, if I could find it out."

"It means," returned the Bigwig family, suspecting something of what he said, "honour and glory in the highest, to the highest merit."

"Oh!" said he. And he was glad to hear that.

But, when he looked among the images in iron, marble, bronze, and brass, he failed to find a rather meritorious countryman of his, once the son of a Warwickshire wool-dealer, or any single countryman whomsoever of that kind. He could find none of the men whose knowledge had rescued him and his children from terrific and disfiguring disease, whose boldness had raised his forefathers from the condition of serfs, whose wise fancy had opened a new and high existence to the humblest, whose skill had filled the working man's world with accumulated wonders. Whereas, he did find others whom he knew no good of, and even others whom he knew much ill of.

"Humph!" said he. "I don't quite understand it."

So, he went home, and sat down by his fireside to get it out of his mind.

Now, his fireside was a bare one, all hemmed in by blackened streets; but it was a precious place to him. The hands of his wife were hardened with toil, and she was old before her time; but she was dear to him. His children, stunted in their growth, bore traces of unwholesome nurture; but they had beauty in his sight. Above all other things, it was an earnest desire of this man's soul that his children should be taught. "If I am sometimes misled," said he, "for want of knowledge, at least let them know better, and avoid my mistakes. If it is hard to me to reap the harvest of pleasure and instruction that is stored in books, let it be easier to them."

But, the Bigwig family broke out into violent family quarrels concerning what it was lawful to teach to this man's children. Some of the family insisted on such a thing being primary and indispensable above all other things; and others of the family insisted on such another thing being primary and indispensable above all other things; and the Bigwig family, rent into factions, wrote pamphlets, held convocations, delivered charges, orations, and all varieties of discourses; impounded one another in courts Lay and courts Ecclesiastical; threw dirt, exchanged pummelings, and fell together by the ears in unintelligible animosity. Meanwhile, this man, in his short evening snatches at his fireside, saw the demon Ignorance arise there, and take his children to itself. He saw his daughter perverted into a heavy, slatternly drudge; he saw his son go moping down the ways of low sensuality, to brutality and crime; he saw the dawning light of intelligence in the eyes of his babies so changing into cunning and suspicion, that he could have rather wished them idiots.

"I don't understand this any the better," said he; "but I think it cannot be right. Nay, by the clouded Heaven above me, I protest against this as my wrong!"

Becoming peaceable again (for his passion was usually short-lived, and his nature kind), he looked about him on his Sundays and holidays, and he saw how much monotony and weariness there was, and thence how drunkenness arose with all its train of ruin. Then he appealed to the Bigwig family, and said, "We are a labouring people, and I have a glimmering suspicion in me that labouring people of whatever condition were made by a higher intelligence than yours, as I poorly understand it, to be in need of mental refreshment and recreation. See what we fall into, when we rest without it. Come! Amuse me harmlessly, show me something, give me an escape!"

But, here the Bigwig family fell into a state of uproar absolutely deafening. When some few voices were faintly heard, proposing to show him the wonders of the world, the greatness of creation, the mighty changes of time, the workings of nature and the beauties of art, to show him these things, that is to say, at any period of his life when he could look upon them, there arose among the Bigwigs such roaring and raving, such pulpiting and petitioning, such maundering and memorialising, such name-calling and dirt-throwing, such a shrill wind of parliamentary questioning and feeble replying where "I dare not" waited on "I would" that the poor fellow stood aghast, staring wildly around.

"Have I provoked all this," said he, with his hands to his affrighted ears, "by what was meant to be an innocent request, plainly arising out of my familiar experience, and the common knowledge of all men who choose to open their eyes? I don't understand, and I am not understood. What is to come of such a state of things!"

He was bending over his work, often asking himself the question, when the news began to spread that a pestilence had appeared among the labourers, and was slaying them by thousands. Going forth to look about him, he soon found this to be true. The dying and the dead were mingled in the close and tainted houses among which his life was passed. New poison was distilled into the always murky, always sickening air. The robust and the weak, old age and infancy, the father and the mother, all were stricken down alike.

What means of flight had he? He remained there, where he was, and saw those who were dearest to him die. A kind preacher came to him, and would have said some prayers to soften his heart in his gloom, but he replied:

"O what avails it, missionary, to come to me, a man condemned to residence in this foetid place, where every sense bestowed upon me for my delight becomes a torment, and where every minute of my numbered days is new mire added to the heap under which I lie oppressed! But, give me my first glimpse of Heaven, through a little of its light and air; give me pure water; help me to be clean; lighten this heavy atmosphere and heavy life, in which our spirits sink, and we become the indifferent and callous creatures you too often see us; gently and kindly take the bodies of those who die among us, out of the small room where we grow to be so familiar with the awful change that even its sanctity is lost to us; and, Teacher, then I will hear, none know better than you, how willingly, of Him whose thoughts were so much with the poor, and who had compassion for all human sorrow!"

He was at work again, solitary and sad, when his Master came and stood near to him dressed in black. He, also, had suffered heavily. His young wife, his beautiful and good young wife, was dead; so, too, his only child.

"Master, 'tis hard to bear, I know it, but be comforted. I would give you comfort, if I could."

The Master thanked him from his heart, but, said he, "O you labouring men! The calamity began among you. If you had but lived more healthily and decently, I should not be the widowed and bereft mourner that I am this day."

"Master," returned the other, shaking his head, "I have begun to understand a little that most calamities will come from us, as this one did, and that none will stop at our poor doors, until we are united with that great squabbling family yonder, to do the things that are right. We cannot live healthily and decently, unless they who undertook to manage us provide the means. We cannot be instructed unless they will teach us; we cannot be rationally amused, unless they will amuse us; we cannot but have some false gods of our own, while they set up so many of theirs in all the public places. The evil consequences of imperfect instruction, the evil consequences of pernicious neglect, the evil consequences of unnatural restraint and the denial of humanising enjoyments, will all come from us, and none of them will stop with us. They will spread far and wide. They always do; they always have done, just like the pestilence. I understand so much, I think, at last."

But the Master said again, "O you labouring men! How seldom do we ever hear of you, except in connection with some trouble!"

"Master," he replied, "I am Nobody, and little likely to be heard of (nor yet much wanted to be heard of, perhaps), except when there is some trouble. But it never begins with me, and it never can end with me. As sure as Death, it comes down to me, and it goes up from me."

There was so much reason in what he said, that the Bigwig family, getting wind of it, and being horribly frightened by the late desolation, resolved to unite with him to do the things that were right, at all events, so far as the said things were associated with the direct prevention, humanly speaking, of another pestilence. But, as their fear wore off, which it soon began to do, they resumed their falling out among themselves, and did nothing. Consequently the scourge appeared again, low down as before and spread avengingly upward as before, and carried off vast numbers of the brawlers. But not a man among them ever admitted, if in the least degree he ever perceived, that he had anything to do with it.

So Nobody lived and died in the old, old, old way; and this, in the main, is the whole of Nobody's story.

Had he no name, you ask? Perhaps it was Legion. It matters little what his name was. Let us call him Legion.

If you were ever in the Belgian villages near the field of Waterloo, you will have seen, in some quiet little church, a monument erected by faithful companions in arms to the memory of Colonel A, Major B, Captains C, D and E, Lieutenants F and G, Ensigns H, I and J, seven non-commissioned officers, and one hundred and thirty rank and file, who fell in the discharge of their duty on the memorable day. The story of Nobody is the story of the rank and file of the earth. They bear their share of the battle; they have their part in the victory; they fall; they leave no name but in the mass. The march of the proudest of us, leads to the dusty way by which they go. O! Let us think of them this year at the Christmas fire, and not forget them when it is burnt out.

The Streets - Morning

The appearance presented by the streets of London an hour before sunrise, on a summer's morning, is most striking even to the few whose unfortunate pursuits of pleasure, or scarcely less unfortunate pursuits of business, cause them to be well acquainted with the scene. There is an air of cold, solitary desolation about the noiseless streets which we are accustomed to see thronged at other times by a busy, eager crowd, and over the quiet, closely- shut buildings, which throughout the day are swarming with life and bustle, that is very impressive.

The last drunken man, who shall find his way home before sunlight, has just staggered heavily along, roaring out the burden of the drinking song of the previous night: the last houseless vagrant whom penury and police have left in the streets, has coiled up his chilly limbs in some paved comer, to dream of food and warmth. The drunken, the dissipated, and the wretched have disappeared; the more sober and orderly part of the population have not yet awakened to the labours of the day, and the stillness of death is over the streets; its very hue seems to be imparted to them, cold and lifeless as they look in the grey, sombre light of daybreak. The coach-stands in the larger thoroughfares are deserted: the night- houses are closed; and the chosen promenades of profligate misery are empty.

An occasional policeman may alone be seen at the street corners, listlessly gazing on the deserted prospect before him; and now and then a rakish-looking cat runs stealthily across the road and descends his own area with as much caution and slyness, bounding first on the water-butt, then on the dust-hole, and then alighting on the flag-stones, as if he were conscious that his character depended on his gallantry of the preceding night escaping public observation. A partially opened bedroom-window here and there, bespeaks the heat of the weather, and the uneasy slumbers of its occupant; and the dim scanty flicker of the rushlight, through the window-blind, denotes the chamber of watching or sickness. With these few exceptions, the streets present no signs of life, nor the houses of habitation.

An hour wears away; the spires of the churches and roofs of the principal buildings are faintly tinged with the light of the rising sun; and the streets, by almost imperceptible degrees, begin to resume their bustle and animation. Market-carts roll slowly along: the sleepy waggoner impatiently urging on his tired horses, or vainly endeavouring to awaken the boy, who, luxuriously stretched on the top of the fruit-baskets, forgets, in happy oblivion, his long-cherished curiosity to behold the wonders of London.

Rough, sleepy-looking animals of strange appearance, something between ostlers and hackney-coachmen, begin to take down the shutters of early public-houses; and little deal tables, with the ordinary preparations for a street breakfast, make their appearance at the customary stations. Numbers of men and women (principally the latter), carrying upon their heads heavy baskets of fruit, toil down the park side of Piccadilly, on their way to Covent-garden, and, following each other in rapid succession, form a long straggling line from thence to the turn of the road at Knightsbridge.

Here and there, a bricklayer's labourer, with the day's dinner tied up in a handkerchief, walks briskly to his work, and occasionally a little knot of three or four schoolboys on a stolen bathing expedition rattle merrily over the pavement, their boisterous mirth contrasting forcibly with the demeanour of the little sweep, who, having knocked and rung till his arm aches, and being interdicted by a merciful legislature from endangering his lungs by calling out, sits patiently down on the door-step, until the housemaid may happen to awake.

Covent-garden market, and the avenues leading to it, are thronged with carts of all sorts, sizes, and descriptions, from the heavy lumbering waggon, with its four stout horses, to the jingling costermonger's cart, with its consumptive donkey. The pavement is already strewed with decayed cabbage-leaves, broken hay-bands, and all the indescribable litter of a vegetable market; men are shouting, carts backing, horses neighing, boys fighting, basket- women talking, piemen expatiating on the excellence of their pastry, and donkeys braying. These and a hundred other sounds form a compound discordant enough to a Londoner's ears, and remarkably disagreeable to those of country gentlemen who are sleeping at the Hummums for the first time.

Another hour passes away, and the day begins in good earnest. The servant of all work, who, under the plea of sleeping very soundly, has utterly disregarded 'Missis's' ringing for half an hour previously, is warned by Master (whom Missis has sent up in his drapery to the landing-place for that purpose), that it's half-past six, whereupon she awakes all of a sudden, with well-feigned astonishment, and goes down-stairs very sulkily, wishing, while she strikes a light, that the principle of spontaneous combustion would extend itself to coals and kitchen range. When the fire is lighted, she opens the street-door to take in the milk, when, by the most singular coincidence in the world, she discovers that the servant next door has just taken in her milk too, and that Mr. Todd's young man over the way, is, by an equally extraordinary chance, taking down his master's shutters. The inevitable consequence is, that she just steps, milk-jug in hand, as far as next door, just to say 'good morning' to Betsy Clark, and that Mr. Todd's young man just steps over the way to say 'good morning' to both of 'em; and as the aforesaid Mr. Todd's young man is almost as good-looking and fascinating as the baker himself, the conversation quickly becomes very interesting, and probably would become more so, if Betsy Clark's Missis, who always will be a-followin' her about, didn't give an angry tap at her bedroom window, on which Mr. Todd's young man tries to whistle coolly, as he goes back to his shop much faster than he came from it; and the two girls run back to their respective places, and shut their street-doors with surprising softness, each of them poking their heads out of the front parlour window, a minute afterwards, however, ostensibly with the view of looking at the mail which just then passes by, but really for the purpose of catching another glimpse of Mr. Todd's young man, who being fond of mails, but more of females, takes a short look at the mails, and a long look at the girls, much to the satisfaction of all parties concerned.

The mail itself goes on to the coach-office in due course, and the passengers who are going out by the early coach, stare with astonishment at the passengers who are coming in by the early coach, who look blue and dismal, and are evidently under the influence of that odd feeling produced by travelling, which makes the events of yesterday morning seem as if they had happened at least six months ago, and induces people to wonder with considerable gravity whether the friends and relations they took leave of a fortnight before, have altered much since they have left them. The coach-office is all alive, and the coaches which are just going out, are surrounded by the usual crowd of Jews and nondescripts, who seem to consider, Heaven knows why, that it is quite impossible any man can mount a coach without requiring at least sixpenny-worth of oranges, a penknife, a pocket-book, a last year's annual, a pencil-case, a piece of sponge, and a small series of caricatures.

Half an hour more, and the sun darts his bright rays cheerfully down the still half-empty streets, and shines with sufficient force to rouse the dismal laziness of the apprentice, who pauses every other minute from his task of sweeping out the shop and watering the pavement in front of it, to tell another apprentice similarly employed, how hot it will be to-day, or to stand with his right hand shading his eyes, and his left resting on the broom, gazing at the 'Wonder,' or the 'Tally-ho,' or the 'Nimrod,' or some other fast coach, till it is out of sight, when he re-enters the shop, envying the passengers on the outside of the fast coach, and thinking of the old red brick house 'down in the country,' where he went to school: the miseries of the milk and water, and thick bread and scrapings, fading into nothing before the pleasant recollection of the green field the boys used to play in, and the green pond he was caned for presuming to fall into, and other schoolboy associations.

Cabs, with trunks and band-boxes between the drivers' legs and outside the apron, rattle briskly up and down the streets on their way to the coach-offices or steam-packet wharfs; and the cab- drivers and hackney-coachmen who are on the stand polish up the ornamental part of their dingy vehicles, the former wondering how people can prefer 'them wild beast cariwans of homnibuses, to a riglar cab with a fast trotter,' and the latter admiring how people can trust their necks into one of 'them crazy cabs, when they can have a 'spectable 'ackney cotche with a pair of 'orses as von't run away with no vun;' a consolation unquestionably founded on fact, seeing that a hackney-coach horse never was known to run at all, 'except,' as the smart cabman in front of the rank observes, 'except one, and HE run back'ards.'

The shops are now completely opened, and apprentices and shopmen are busily engaged in cleaning and decking the windows for the day. The bakers' shops in town are filled with servants and children waiting for the drawing of the first batch of rolls, an operation which was performed a full hour ago in the suburbs: for the early clerk population of Somers and Camden towns, Islington, and Pentonville, are fast pouring into the city, or directing their steps towards Chancery-lane and the Inns of Court. Middle-aged men, whose salaries have by no means increased in the same proportion as their families, plod steadily along, apparently with no object in view but the counting-house; knowing by sight almost everybody they meet or overtake, for they have seen them every morning (Sunday excepted) during the last twenty years, but speaking to no one. If they do happen to overtake a personal acquaintance, they just exchange a hurried salutation, and keep walking on either by his side, or in front of him, as his rate of walking may chance to be. As to stopping to shake hands, or to take the friend's arm, they seem to think that as it is not included in their salary, they have no right to do it. Small office lads in large hats, who are made men before they are boys, hurry along in pairs, with their first coat carefully brushed, and the white trousers of last Sunday plentifully besmeared with dust and ink. It evidently requires a considerable mental struggle to avoid investing part of the day's dinner-money in the purchase of the stale tarts so temptingly exposed in dusty tins at the pastry- cooks' doors; but a consciousness of their own importance and the receipt of seven shillings a-week, with the prospect of an early rise to eight, comes to their aid, and they accordingly put their hats a little more on one side, and look under the bonnets of all the milliners' and stay-makers' apprentices they meet, poor girls! the hardest worked, the worst paid, and too often, the worst used class of the community.

Eleven o'clock, and a new set of people fill the streets. The goods in the shop-windows are invitingly arranged; the shopmen in their white neckerchiefs and spruce coats, look as it they couldn't clean a window if their lives depended on it; the carts have disappeared from Covent-garden; the waggoners have returned, and the costermongers repaired to their ordinary 'beats' in the suburbs; clerks are at their offices, and gigs, cabs, omnibuses, and saddle-horses, are conveying their masters to the same destination. The streets are thronged with a vast concourse of people, gay and shabby, rich and poor, idle and industrious; and we come to the heat, bustle, and activity of NOON.

The Begging-Letter Writer

THE amount of money he annually diverts from wholesome and useful purposes in the United Kingdom, would be a set-off against the Window Tax. He is one of the most shameless frauds and impositions of this time. In his idleness, his mendacity, and the immeasurable harm he does to the deserving, - dirtying the stream of true benevolence, and muddling the brains of foolish justices, with inability to distinguish between the base coin of distress, and the true currency we have always among us,

- he is more worthy of Norfolk Island than three-fourths of the worst characters who are sent there. Under any rational system, he would have been sent there long ago.

I, the writer of this paper, have been, for some time, a chosen receiver of Begging Letters. For fourteen years, my house has been made as regular a Receiving House for such communications as any one of the great branch Post-Offices is for general correspondence. I ought to know something of the Begging-Letter Writer. He has besieged my door at all hours of the day and night; he has fought my servant; he has lain in ambush for me, going out and coming in; he has followed me out of town into the country; he has appeared at provincial hotels, where I have been staying for only a few hours; he has written to me from immense distances, when I have been out of England. He has fallen sick; he has died and been buried; he has come to life again, and again departed from this transitory scene: he has been his own son, his own mother, his own baby, his idiot brother, his uncle, his aunt, his aged grandfather. He has wanted a greatcoat, to go to India in; a pound to set him up in life for ever; a pair of boots to take him to the coast of China; a hat to get him into a permanent situation under Government. He has frequently been exactly seven-and-sixpence short of independence. He has had such openings at Liverpool - posts of great trust and confidence in merchants' houses, which nothing but seven-and-sixpence was wanting to him to secure - that I wonder he is not Mayor of that flourishing town at the present moment.

The natural phenomena of which he has been the victim, are of a most astounding nature. He has had two children who have never grown up; who have never had anything to cover them at night; who have been continually driving him mad, by asking in vain for food; who have never come out of fevers and measles (which, I suppose, has accounted for his fuming his letters with tobacco smoke, as a disinfectant); who have never changed in the least degree through fourteen long revolving years. As to his wife, what that suffering woman has undergone, nobody knows. She has always been in an interesting situation through the same long period, and has never been confined yet. His devotion to her has been unceasing. He has never cared for himself; HE could have perished - he would rather, in short - but was it not his Christian duty as a man, a husband, and a father, - to write begging letters when he looked at her? (He has usually remarked that he would call in the evening for an answer to this question.)

He has been the sport of the strangest misfortunes. What his brother has done to him would have broken anybody else's heart. His brother went into business with him, and ran away with the money; his brother got him to be security for an immense sum and left him to pay it; his brother would have given him employment to the tune of hundreds a-year, if he would have consented to write letters on a Sunday; his brother enunciated principles incompatible with his religious views, and he could not (in consequence) permit his brother to provide for him. His landlord has never shown a spark of human feeling. When he put in that execution I don't know, but he has never taken it out. The broker's man has grown grey in possession. They will have to bury him some day.

He has been attached to every conceivable pursuit. He has been in the army, in the navy, in the church, in the law; connected with the press, the fine arts, public institutions, every description and grade of business. He has been brought up as a gentleman; he has been at every college in Oxford and Cambridge; he can quote

Latin in his letters (but generally misspells some minor English word); he can tell you what Shakespeare says about begging, better than you know it. It is to be observed, that in the midst of his afflictions he always reads the newspapers; and rounds off his appeal with some allusion, that may be supposed to be in my way, to the popular subject of the hour.

His life presents a series of inconsistencies. Sometimes he has never written such a letter before. He blushes with shame. That is the first time; that shall be the last. Don't answer it, and let it be understood that, then, he will kill himself quietly. Sometimes (and more frequently) he HAS written a few such letters. Then he encloses the answers, with an intimation that they are of inestimable value to him, and a request that they may be carefully returned. He is fond of enclosing something - verses, letters, pawnbrokers' duplicates, anything to necessitate an answer. He is very severe upon 'the pampered minion of fortune,' who refused him the half-sovereign referred to in the enclosure number two - but he knows me better.

He writes in a variety of styles; sometimes in low spirits; sometimes quite jocosely. When he is in low spirits he writes down-hill and repeats words - these little indications being expressive of the perturbation of his mind. When he is more vivacious, he is frank with me; he is quite the agreeable rattle. I know what human nature is, - who better? Well! He had a little money once, and he ran through it - as many men have done before him. He finds his old friends turn away from him now - many men have done that before him too! Shall he tell me why he writes to me? Because he has no kind of claim upon me. He puts it on that ground plainly; and begs to ask for the loan (as I know human nature) of two sovereigns, to be repaid next Tuesday six weeks, before twelve at noon.

Sometimes, when he is sure that I have found him out, and that there is no chance of money, he writes to inform me that I have got rid of him at last. He has enlisted into the Company's service, and is off directly - but he wants a cheese. He is informed by the serjeant that it is essential to his prospects in the regiment that he should take out a single Gloucester cheese, weighing from twelve to fifteen pounds. Eight or nine shillings would buy it. He does not ask for money, after what has passed; but if he calls at nine, to-morrow morning may he hope to find a cheese? And is there anything he can do to show his gratitude in Bengal?

Once he wrote me rather a special letter, proposing relief in kind. He had got into a little trouble by leaving parcels of mud done up in brown paper, at people's houses, on pretence of being a Railway- Porter, in which character he received carriage money. This sportive fancy he expiated in the House of Correction. Not long after his release, and on a Sunday morning, he called with a letter (having first dusted himself all over), in which he gave me to understand that, being resolved to earn an honest livelihood, he had been travelling about the country with a cart of crockery. That he had been doing pretty well until the day before, when his horse had dropped down dead near Chatham, in Kent. That this had reduced him to the unpleasant necessity of getting into the shafts himself, and drawing the cart of crockery to London - a somewhat exhausting pull of thirty miles. That he did not venture to ask again for money; but that if I would have the goodness TO LEAVE HIM OUT A DONKEY, he would call for the animal before breakfast!

At another time my friend (I am describing actual experiences) introduced himself as a literary gentleman in the last extremity of distress. He had had a play accepted at a certain Theatre - which was really open; its representation was delayed by the indisposition of a leading actor - who was really ill; and he and his were in a state of absolute starvation. If he made his necessities known to the Manager of the Theatre, he put it to me to say what kind of treatment he might expect? Well! we got over that difficulty to our mutual satisfaction. A little while afterwards he was in some other strait. I think Mrs. Southcote, his wife, was in extremity - and we adjusted that point too. A little while afterwards he had taken a new house, and was going headlong to ruin for want of a water-butt. I had my misgivings about the water-butt, and did not reply to that epistle. But a little while afterwards, I had reason to feel penitent for my neglect. He wrote me a few broken-hearted lines, informing me that the dear partner of his sorrows died in his arms last night at nine o'clock!

I despatched a trusty messenger to comfort the bereaved mourner and his poor children; but the messenger went so soon, that the play was not ready to be played out; my friend was not at home, and his wife was in a most delightful state of health. He was taken up by the Mendicity Society (informally it afterwards appeared), and I presented myself at a London Police-Office with my testimony against him. The Magistrate was wonderfully struck by his educational acquirements, deeply impressed by the excellence of his letters, exceedingly sorry to see a man of his attainments there, complimented him highly on his powers of composition, and was quite charmed to have the agreeable duty of discharging him. A collection was made for the 'poor fellow,' as he was called in the reports, and I left the court with a comfortable sense of being universally regarded as a sort of monster. Next day comes to me a friend of mine, the governor of a large prison. 'Why did you ever go to the Police-Office against that man,' says he, 'without coming to me first? I know all about him and his frauds. He lodged in the house of one of my warders, at the very time when he first wrote to you; and then he was eating spring-lamb at eighteen-pence a pound, and early asparagus at I don't know how much a bundle!' On that very same day, and in that very same hour, my injured gentleman wrote a solemn address to me, demanding to know what compensation I proposed to make him for his having passed the night in a 'loathsome dungeon.' And next morning an Irish gentleman, a member of the same fraternity, who had read the case, and was very well persuaded I should be chary of going to that Police-Office again, positively refused to leave my door for less than a sovereign, and, resolved to besiege me into compliance, literally 'sat down' before it for ten mortal hours. The garrison being well provisioned, I remained within the walls; and he raised the siege at midnight with a prodigious alarum on the bell.

The Begging-Letter Writer often has an extensive circle of acquaintance. Whole pages of the 'Court Guide' are ready to be references for him. Noblemen and gentlemen write to say there never was such a man for probity and virtue. They have known him time out of mind, and there is nothing they wouldn't do for him. Somehow, they don't give him that one pound ten he stands in need of; but perhaps it is not enough - they want to do more, and his modesty will not allow it. It is to be remarked of his trade that it is a very fascinating one. He never leaves it; and those who are near to him become smitten with a love of it, too, and sooner or later set up for themselves. He employs a messenger - man, woman, or child. That messenger is certain ultimately to become an independent Begging-Letter Writer. His sons and daughters succeed to his calling, and write begging-letters when he is no more. He throws off the infection of begging-letter writing, like the contagion of disease. What Sydney Smith so happily called 'the dangerous luxury of dishonesty' is more tempting, and more catching, it would seem, in this instance than in any other.

He always belongs to a Corresponding-Society of Begging-Letter Writers. Any one who will, may ascertain this fact. Give money to-day in recognition of a begging-letter, - no matter how unlike a common begging-letter, - and for the next fortnight you will have a rush of such communications. Steadily refuse to give; and the begging-letters become Angels' visits, until the Society is from some cause or other in a dull way of business, and may as well try you as anybody else. It is of little use inquiring into the Begging-Letter Writer's circumstances. He may be sometimes accidentally found out, as in the case already mentioned (though that was not the first inquiry made); but apparent misery is always a part of his trade, and real misery very often is, in the intervals of spring-lamb and early asparagus. It is naturally an incident of his dissipated and dishonest life.

That the calling is a successful one, and that large sums of money are gained by it, must be evident to anybody who reads the Police Reports of such cases. But, prosecutions are of rare occurrence, relatively to the extent to which the trade is carried on. The cause of this is to be found (as no one knows better than the Begging-Letter Writer, for it is a part of his speculation) in the aversion people feel to exhibit themselves as having been imposed upon, or as having weakly gratified their consciences with a lazy, flimsy substitute for the noblest of all virtues. There is a man at large, at the moment when this paper is preparing for the press (on the 29th of April, 1850), and never once taken up yet, who, within these twelvemonths, has been probably the most audacious and the most successful swindler that even this trade has ever known. There has been something singularly base in this fellow's proceedings; it has been his business to write to all sorts and conditions of people, in the names of persons of high reputation and unblemished honour, professing to be in distress - the general admiration and respect for whom has ensured a ready and generous reply.

Now, in the hope that the results of the real experience of a real person may do something more to induce reflection on this subject than any abstract treatise - and with a personal knowledge of the extent to which the Begging-Letter Trade has been carried on for some time, and has been for some time constantly increasing - the writer of this paper entreats the attention of his readers to a few concluding words. His experience is a type of the experience of many; some on a smaller, some on an infinitely larger scale. All may judge of the soundness or unsoundness of his conclusions from it.

Long doubtful of the efficacy of such assistance in any case whatever, and able to recall but one, within his whole individual knowledge, in which he had the least after-reason to suppose that any good was done by it, he was led, last autumn, into some serious considerations. The begging-letters flying about by every post, made it perfectly manifest that a set of lazy vagabonds were interposed between the general desire to do something to relieve the sickness and misery under which the poor were suffering, and the suffering poor themselves. That many who sought to do some little to repair the social wrongs, inflicted in the way of preventible sickness and death upon the poor, were strengthening those wrongs, however innocently, by wasting money on pestilent knaves cumbering society. That imagination, - soberly following one of these knaves into his life of punishment in jail, and comparing it with the life of one of these poor in a cholera- stricken alley, or one of the children of one of these poor, soothed in its dying hour by the late lamented Mr. Drouet, - contemplated a grim farce, impossible to be presented very much longer before God or man. That the crowning miracle of all the miracles summed up in the New Testament, after the miracle of the blind seeing, and the lame walking, and the restoration of the dead to life, was the miracle that the poor had the Gospel preached to them. That while the poor were unnaturally and unnecessarily cut off by the thousand, in the prematurity of their age, or in the rottenness of their youth - for of flower or blossom such youth has none - the Gospel was NOT preached to them, saving in hollow and unmeaning voices. That of all wrongs, this was the first mighty wrong the Pestilence warned us to set right. And that no Post- Office Order to any amount, given to a Begging-Letter Writer for the quieting of an uneasy breast, would be presentable on the Last Great Day as anything towards it.

The poor never write these letters. Nothing could be more unlike their habits. The writers are public robbers; and we who support them are parties to their depredations. They trade upon every circumstance within their knowledge that affects us, public or private, joyful or sorrowful; they pervert the lessons of our lives; they change what ought to be our strength and virtue into weakness, and encouragement of vice. There is a plain remedy, and it is in our own hands. We must resolve, at any sacrifice of feeling, to be deaf to such appeals, and crush the trade.

There are degrees in murder. Life must be held sacred among us in more ways than one - sacred, not merely from the murderous weapon, or the subtle poison, or the cruel blow, but sacred from preventitive diseases, distortions, and pains. That is the first great end we have to set against this miserable imposition. Physical life respected, moral life comes next. What will not content a Begging-Letter Writer for a week, would educate a score of children for a year. Let us give all we can; let us give more than ever. Let us do all we can; let us do more than ever. But let us give, and do, with a high purpose; not to endow the scum of the earth, to its own greater corruption, with the offals of our duty.

The Drunkard's Death

We will be bold to say, that there is scarcely a man in the constant habit of walking, day after day, through any of the crowded thoroughfares of London, who cannot recollect among the people whom he 'knows by sight,' to use a familiar phrase, some being of abject and wretched appearance whom he remembers to have seen in a very different condition, whom he has observed sinking lower and lower, by almost imperceptible degrees, and the shabbiness and utter destitution of whose appearance, at last, strike forcibly and painfully upon him, as he passes by. Is there any man who has mixed much with society, or whose avocations have caused him to mingle, at one time or other, with a great number of people, who cannot call to mind the time when some shabby, miserable wretch, in rags and filth, who shuffles past him now in all the squalor of disease and poverty, with a respectable tradesman, or clerk, or a man following some thriving pursuit, with good prospects, and decent means? or cannot any of our readers call to mind from among the list of their quondam acquaintance, some fallen and degraded man, who lingers about the pavement in hungry misery, from whom every one turns coldly away, and who preserves himself from sheer starvation, nobody knows how? Alas! such cases are of too frequent occurrence to be rare items in any man's experience; and but too often arise from one cause: drunkenness, that fierce rage for the slow, sure poison, that oversteps every other consideration; that casts aside wife, children, friends, happiness, and station; and hurries its victims madly on to degradation and death.

Some of these men have been impelled, by misfortune and misery, to the vice that has degraded them. The ruin of worldly expectations, the death of those they loved, the sorrow that slowly consumes, but will not break the heart, has driven them wild; and they present the hideous spectacle of madmen, slowly dying by their own hands. But by far the greater part have wilfully, and with open eyes, plunged into the gulf from which the man who once enters it never rises more, but into which he sinks deeper and deeper down, until recovery is hopeless.

Such a man as this once stood by the bedside of his dying wife, while his children knelt around, and mingled loud bursts of grief with their innocent prayers. The room was scantily and meanly furnished; and it needed but a glance at the pale form from which the light of life was fast passing away, to know that grief, and want, and anxious care, had been busy at the heart for many a weary year. An elderly woman, with her face bathed in tears, was supporting the head of the dying woman, her daughter on her arm. But it was not towards her that the was face turned; it was not her hand that the cold and trembling fingers clasped; they pressed the husband's arm; the eyes so soon to be closed in death rested on his face, and the man shook beneath their gaze. His dress was slovenly and disordered, his face inflamed, his eyes bloodshot and heavy. He had been summoned from some wild debauch to the bed of sorrow and death.

A shaded lamp by the bed-side cast a dim light on the figures around, and left the remainder of the room in thick, deep shadow. The silence of night prevailed without the house, and the stillness of death was in the chamber. A watch hung over the mantel-shelf; its low ticking was the only sound that broke the profound quiet, but it was a solemn one, for well they knew, who heard it, that before it had recorded the passing of another hour, it would beat the knell of a departed spirit.

It is a dreadful thing to wait and watch for the approach of death; to know that hope is gone, and recovery impossible; and to sit and count the dreary hours through long, long nights, such nights as only watchers by the bed of sickness know. It chills the blood to hear the dearest secrets of the heart, the pent-up, hidden secrets of many years, poured forth by the unconscious, helpless being before you; and to think how little the reserve and cunning of a whole life will avail, when fever and delirium tear off the mask at last. Strange tales have been told in the wanderings of dying men; tales so full of guilt and crime, that those who stood by the sick person's couch have fled in horror and affright, lest they should be scared to madness by what they heard and saw; and many a wretch has died alone, raving of deeds the very name of which has driven the boldest man away.

But no such ravings were to be heard at the bed-side by which the children knelt. Their half-stifled sobs and moaning alone broke the silence of the lonely chamber.

And when at last the mother's grasp relaxed, and, turning one look from the children to the father, she vainly strove to speak, and fell backward on the pillow, all was so calm and tranquil that she seemed to sink to sleep. They leant over her; they called upon her name, softly at first, and then in the loud and piercing tones of desperation. But there was no reply. They listened for her breath, but no sound came. They felt for the palpitation of the heart, but no faint throb responded to the touch. That heart was broken, and she was dead!

The husband sunk into a chair by the bed-side, and clasped his hands upon his burning forehead. He gazed from child to child, but when a weeping eye met his, he quailed beneath its look. No word of comfort was whispered in his ear, no look of kindness lighted on his face. All shrunk from and avoided him; and when at last he staggered from the room, no one sought to follow or console the widower.

The time had been when many a friend would have crowded round him in his affliction, and many a heartfelt condolence would have met him in his grief. Where were they now? One by one, friends, relations, the commonest acquaintance even, had fallen off from and deserted the drunkard. His wife alone had clung to him in good and evil, in sickness and poverty, and how had he rewarded her? He had reeled from the tavern to her bed-side in time to see her die.

He rushed from the house, and walked swiftly through the streets. Remorse, fear, shame, all crowded on his mind. Stupefied with drink, and bewildered with the scene he had just witnessed, he re- entered the tavern he had quitted shortly before. Glass succeeded glass. His blood mounted, and his brain whirled round. Death! Every one must die, and why not SHE? She was too good for him; her relations had often told him so. Curses on them! Had they not deserted her, and left her to whine away the time at home? Well, she was dead, and happy perhaps. It was better as it was. Another glass, one more! Hurrah! It was a merry life while it lasted; and he would make the most of it.

Time went on; the three children who were left to him, grew up, and were children no longer. The father remained the same, poorer, shabbier, and more dissolute-looking, but the same confirmed and irreclaimable drunkard. The boys had, long ago, run wild in the streets, and left him; the girl alone remained, but she worked hard, and words or blows could always procure him something for the tavern. So he went on in the old course, and a merry life he led.

One night, as early as ten o'clock, for the girl had been sick for many days, and there was, consequently, little to spend at the public-house, he bent his steps homeward, bethinking himself that if he would have her able to earn money, it would be as well to apply to the parish surgeon, or, at all events, to take the trouble of inquiring what ailed her, which he had not yet thought it worth while to do. It was a wet December night; the wind blew piercing cold, and the rain poured heavily down. He begged a few halfpence from a passer-by, and having bought a small loaf (for it was his interest to keep the girl alive, if he could), he shuffled onwards as fast as the wind and rain would let him.

At the back of Fleet-street, and lying between it and the water- side, are several mean and narrow courts, which form a portion of Whitefriars: it was to one of these that he directed his steps.

The alley into which he turned, might, for filth and misery, have competed with the darkest corner of this ancient sanctuary in its dirtiest and most lawless time. The houses, varying from two stories in height to four, were stained with every indescribable hue that long exposure to the weather, damp, and rottenness can impart to tenements composed originally of the roughest and coarsest materials. The windows were patched with paper, and stuffed with the foulest rags; the doors were falling from their hinges; poles with lines on which to dry clothes, projected from every casement, and sounds of quarrelling or drunkenness issued from every room.

The solitary oil lamp in the centre of the court had been blown out, either by the violence of the wind or the act of some inhabitant who had excellent reasons for objecting to his residence being rendered too conspicuous; and the only light which fell upon the broken and uneven pavement, was derived from the miserable candles that here and there twinkled in the rooms of such of the more fortunate residents as could afford to indulge in so expensive a luxury. A gutter ran down the centre of the alley, all the sluggish odours of which had been called forth by the rain; and as the wind whistled through the old houses, the doors and shutters creaked upon their hinges, and the windows shook in their frames, with a violence which every moment seemed to threaten the destruction of the whole place.

The man whom we have followed into this den, walked on in the darkness, sometimes stumbling into the main gutter, and at others into some branch repositories of garbage which had been formed by the rain, until he reached the last house in the court. The door, or rather what was left of it, stood ajar, for the convenience of the numerous lodgers; and he proceeded to grope his way up the old and broken stair, to the attic story.

He was within a step or two of his room door, when it opened, and a girl, whose miserable and emaciated appearance was only to be equalled by that of the candle which she shaded with her hand, peeped anxiously out.

'Is that you, father?' said the girl.

'Who else should it be?' replied the man gruffly. 'What are you trembling at? It's little enough that I've had to drink to-day, for there's no drink without money, and no money without work. What the devil's the matter with the girl?'

'I am not well, father, not at all well,' said the girl, bursting into tears.

'Ah!' replied the man, in the tone of a person who is compelled to admit a very unpleasant fact, to which he would rather remain blind, if he could. 'You must get better somehow, for we must have money. You must go to the parish doctor, and make him give you some medicine. They're paid for it, damn 'em. What are you standing before the door for? Let me come in, can't you?'

'Father,' whispered the girl, shutting the door behind her, and placing herself before it, 'William has come back.'

'Who!' said the man with a start.

'Hush,' replied the girl, 'William; brother William.'

'And what does he want?' said the man, with an effort at composure, 'money? meat? drink? He's come to the wrong shop for that, if he does. Give me the candle, give me the candle, fool, I ain't going to hurt him.' He snatched the candle from her hand, and walked into the room.

Sitting on an old box, with his head resting on his hand, and his eyes fixed on a wretched cinder fire that was smouldering on the hearth, was a young man of about two-and-twenty, miserably clad in an old coarse jacket and trousers. He started up when his father entered.

'Fasten the door, Mary,' said the young man hastily. 'Fasten the door. You look as if you didn't know me, father. It's long enough, since you drove me from home; you may well forget me.'

'And what do you want here, now?' said the father, seating himself on a stool, on the other side of the fireplace. 'What do you want here, now?'

'Shelter,' replied the son. 'I'm in trouble: that's enough. If I'm caught I shall swing; that's certain. Caught I shall be, unless I stop here; that's AS certain. And there's an end of it.'

'You mean to say, you've been robbing, or murdering, then?' said the father.

'Yes, I do,' replied the son. 'Does it surprise you, father?' He looked steadily in the man's face, but he withdrew his eyes, and bent them on the ground.

'Where's your brothers?' he said, after a long pause.

'Where they'll never trouble you,' replied his son: 'John's gone to America, and Henry's dead.'

'Dead!' said the father, with a shudder, which even he could not express.

'Dead,' replied the young man. 'He died in my arms, shot like a dog, by a gamekeeper. He staggered back, I caught him, and his blood trickled down my hands. It poured out from his side like water. He was weak, and it blinded him, but he threw himself down on his knees, on the grass, and prayed to God, that if his mother was in heaven, He would hear her prayers for pardon for her youngest son. "I was her favourite boy, Will," he said, "and I am glad to think, now, that when she was dying, though I was a very young child then, and my little heart was almost bursting, I knelt down at the foot of the bed, and thanked God for having made me so fond of her as to have never once done anything to bring the tears into her eyes. O Will, why was she taken away, and father left?" There's his dying words, father,' said the young man; 'make the best you can of 'em. You struck him across the face, in a drunken fit, the morning we ran away; and here's the end of it.'

The girl wept aloud; and the father, sinking his head upon his knees, rocked himself to and fro.

'If I am taken,' said the young man, 'I shall be carried back into the country, and hung for that man's murder. They cannot trace me here, without your assistance, father. For aught I know, you may give me up to justice; but unless you do, here I stop, until I can venture to escape abroad.'

For two whole days, all three remained in the wretched room, without stirring out. On the third evening, however, the girl was worse than she had been yet, and the few scraps of food they had were gone. It was indispensably necessary that somebody should go out; and as the girl was too weak and ill, the father went, just at nightfall.

He got some medicine for the girl, and a trifle in the way of pecuniary assistance. On his way back, he earned sixpence by holding a horse; and he turned homewards with enough money to supply their most pressing wants for two or three days to come. He had to pass the public-house. He lingered for an instant, walked past it, turned back again, lingered once more, and finally slunk in. Two men whom he had not observed, were on the watch. They were on the point of giving up their search in despair, when his loitering attracted their attention; and when he entered the public-house, they followed him.

'You'll drink with me, master,' said one of them, proffering him a glass of liquor.

'And me too,' said the other, replenishing the glass as soon as it was drained of its contents.

The man thought of his hungry children, and his son's danger. But they were nothing to the drunkard. He DID drink; and his reason left him.

'A wet night, Warden,' whispered one of the men in his ear, as he at length turned to go away, after spending in liquor one-half of the money on which, perhaps, his daughter's life depended.

'The right sort of night for our friends in hiding, Master Warden,' whispered the other.

'Sit down here,' said the one who had spoken first, drawing him into a corner. 'We have been looking arter the young un. We came to tell him, it's all right now, but we couldn't find him 'cause we hadn't got the precise direction. But that ain't strange, for I don't think he know'd it himself, when he come to London, did he?'

'No, he didn't,' replied the father.

The two men exchanged glances.

'There's a vessel down at the docks, to sail at midnight, when it's high water,' resumed the first speaker, 'and we'll put him on board. His passage is taken in another name, and what's better than that, it's paid for. It's lucky we met you.'

'Very,' said the second.

'Capital luck,' said the first, with a wink to his companion.

'Great,' replied the second, with a slight nod of intelligence.

'Another glass here; quick', said the first speaker. And in five minutes more, the father had unconsciously yielded up his own son into the hangman's hands.

Slowly and heavily the time dragged along, as the brother and sister, in their miserable hiding-place, listened in anxious suspense to the slightest sound. At length, a heavy footstep was heard upon the stair; it approached nearer; it reached the landing; and the father staggered into the room.

The girl saw that he was intoxicated, and advanced with the candle in her hand to meet him; she stopped short, gave a loud scream, and fell senseless on the ground. She had caught sight of the shadow of a man reflected on the floor. They both rushed in, and in another instant the young man was a prisoner, and handcuffed.

'Very quietly done,' said one of the men to his companion, 'thanks to the old man. Lift up the girl, Tom, come, come, it's no use crying, young woman. It's all over now, and can't be helped.'

The young man stooped for an instant over the girl, and then turned fiercely round upon his father, who had reeled against the wall, and was gazing on the group with drunken stupidity.

'Listen to me, father,' he said, in a tone that made the drunkard's flesh creep. 'My brother's blood, and mine, is on your head: I never had kind look, or word, or care, from you, and alive or dead, I never will forgive you. Die when you will, or how, I will be with you. I speak as a dead man now, and I warn you, father, that as surely as you must one day stand before your Maker, so surely shall your children be there, hand in hand, to cry for judgment against you.' He raised his manacled hands in a threatening attitude, fixed his eyes on his shrinking parent, and slowly left the room; and neither father nor sister ever beheld him more, on this side of the grave.

When the dim and misty light of a winter's morning penetrated into the narrow court, and struggled through the begrimed window of the wretched room, Warden awoke from his heavy sleep, and found himself alone. He rose, and looked round him; the old flock mattress on the floor was undisturbed; everything was just as he remembered to have seen it last: and there were no signs of any one, save himself, having occupied the room during the night. He inquired of the other lodgers, and of the neighbours; but his daughter had not been seen or heard of. He rambled through the streets, and scrutinised each wretched face among the crowds that thronged them, with anxious eyes. But his search was fruitless, and he returned to his garret when night came on, desolate and weary.

For many days he occupied himself in the same manner, but no trace of his daughter did he meet with, and no word of her reached his ears. At length he gave up the pursuit as hopeless. He had long thought of the probability of her leaving him, and endeavouring to gain her bread in quiet, elsewhere. She had left him at last to starve alone. He ground his teeth, and cursed her!

He begged his bread from door to door. Every halfpenny he could wring from the pity or credulity of those to whom he addressed himself, was spent in the old way. A year passed over his head; the roof of a jail was the only one that had sheltered him for many months. He slept under archways, and in brickfields, anywhere, where there was some warmth or shelter from the cold and rain. But in the last stage of poverty, disease, and houseless want, he was a drunkard still.

At last, one bitter night, he sunk down on a door-step faint and ill. The premature decay of vice and profligacy had worn him to the bone. His cheeks were hollow and livid; his eyes were sunken, and their sight was dim. His legs trembled beneath his weight, and a cold shiver ran through every limb.

And now the long-forgotten scenes of a misspent life crowded thick and fast upon him. He thought of the time when he had a home, a happy, cheerful home, and of those who peopled it, and flocked about him then, until the forms of his elder children seemed to rise from the grave, and stand about him, so plain, so clear, and so distinct they were that he could touch and feel them. Looks that he had long forgotten were fixed upon him once more; voices long since hushed in death sounded in his ears like the music of village bells. But it was only for an instant. The rain beat heavily upon him; and cold and hunger were gnawing at his heart again.

He rose, and dragged his feeble limbs a few paces further. The street was silent and empty; the few passengers who passed by, at that late hour, hurried quickly on, and his tremulous voice was lost in the violence of the storm. Again that heavy chill struck through his frame, and his blood seemed to stagnate beneath it. He coiled himself up in a projecting doorway, and tried to sleep.

But sleep had fled from his dull and glazed eyes. His mind wandered strangely, but he was awake, and conscious. The well- known shout of drunken mirth sounded in his ear, the glass was at his lips, the board was covered with choice rich food, they were before him: he could see them all, he had but to reach out his hand, and take them, and, though the illusion was reality itself, he knew that he was sitting alone in the deserted street, watching the rain-drops as they pattered on the stones; that death was coming upon him by inches, and that there were none to care for or help him.

Suddenly he started up, in the extremity of terror. He had heard his own voice shouting in the night air, he knew not what, or why. Hark! A groan! another! His senses were leaving him: half- formed and incoherent words burst from his lips; and his hands sought to tear and lacerate his flesh. He was going mad, and he shrieked for help till his voice failed him.

He raised his head, and looked up the long dismal street. He recollected that outcasts like himself, condemned to wander day and night in those dreadful streets, had sometimes gone distracted with their own loneliness. He remembered to have heard many years before that a homeless wretch had once been found in a solitary corner, sharpening a rusty knife to plunge into his own heart, preferring death to that endless, weary, wandering to and fro. In an instant his resolve was taken, his limbs received new life; he ran quickly from the spot, and paused not for breath until he reached the river-side.

He crept softly down the steep stone stairs that lead from the commencement of Waterloo Bridge, down to the water's level. He crouched into a corner, and held his breath, as the patrol passed. Never did prisoner's heart throb with the hope of liberty and life half so eagerly as did that of the wretched man at the prospect of death. The watch passed close to him, but he remained unobserved; and after waiting till the sound of footsteps had died away in the distance, he cautiously descended, and stood beneath the gloomy arch that forms the landing-place from the river.

The tide was in, and the water flowed at his feet. The rain had ceased, the wind was lulled, and all was, for the moment, still and quiet, so quiet, that the slightest sound on the opposite bank, even the rippling of the water against the barges that were moored there, was distinctly audible to his ear. The stream stole languidly and sluggishly on. Strange and fantastic forms rose to the surface, and beckoned him to approach; dark gleaming eyes peered from the water, and seemed to mock his hesitation, while hollow murmurs from behind, urged him onwards. He retreated a few paces, took a short run, desperate leap, and plunged into the river.

Not five seconds had passed when he rose to the water's surface but what a change had taken place in that short time, in all his thoughts and feelings! Life, life in any form, poverty, misery, starvation, anything but death. He fought and struggled with the water that closed over his head, and screamed in agonies of terror. The curse of his own son rang in his ears. The shore, but one foot of dry ground, he could almost touch the step. One hand's breadth nearer, and he was saved, but the tide bore him onward, under the dark arches of the bridge, and he sank to the bottom.

Again he rose, and struggled for life. For one instant, for one brief instant, the buildings on the river's banks, the lights on the bridge through which the current had borne him, the black water, and the fast-flying clouds, were distinctly visible, once more he sunk, and once again he rose. Bright flames of fire shot up from earth to heaven, and reeled before his eyes, while the water thundered in his ears, and stunned him with its furious roar.

A week afterwards the body was washed ashore, some miles down the river, a swollen and disfigured mass. Unrecognised and unpitied, it was borne to the grave; and there it has long since mouldered away!

Gin-Shops

It is a remarkable circumstance, that different trades appear to partake of the disease to which elephants and dogs are especially liable, and to run stark, staring, raving mad, periodically. The great distinction between the animals and the trades, is, that the former run mad with a certain degree of propriety, they are very regular in their irregularities. We know the period at which the emergency will arise, and provide against it accordingly. If an elephant run mad, we are all ready for him, kill or cure, pills or bullets, calomel in conserve of roses, or lead in a musket-barrel. If a dog happen to look unpleasantly warm in the summer months, and to trot about the shady side of the streets with a quarter of a yard of tongue hanging out of his mouth, a thick leather muzzle, which has been previously prepared in compliance with the thoughtful injunctions of the Legislature, is instantly clapped over his head, by way of making him cooler, and he either looks remarkably unhappy for the next six weeks, or becomes legally insane, and goes mad, as it were, by Act of Parliament. But these trades are as eccentric as comets; nay, worse, for no one can calculate on the recurrence of the strange appearances which betoken the disease. Moreover, the contagion is general, and the quickness with which it diffuses itself, almost incredible.

We will cite two or three cases in illustration of our meaning. Six or eight years ago, the epidemic began to display itself among the linen-drapers and haberdashers. The primary symptoms were an inordinate love of plate-glass, and a passion for gas-lights and gilding. The disease gradually progressed, and at last attained a fearful height. Quiet, dusty old shops in different parts of town, were pulled down; spacious premises with stuccoed fronts and gold letters, were erected instead; floors were covered with Turkey carpets; roofs supported by massive pillars; doors knocked into windows; a dozen squares of glass into one; one shopman into a dozen; and there is no knowing what would have been done, if it had not been fortunately discovered, just in time, that the Commissioners of Bankruptcy were as competent to decide such cases as the Commissioners of Lunacy, and that a little confinement and gentle examination did wonders. The disease abated. It died away. A year or two of comparative tranquillity ensued. Suddenly it burst out again amongst the chemists; the symptoms were the same, with the addition of a strong desire to stick the royal arms over the shop-door, and a great rage for mahogany, varnish, and expensive floor-cloth. Then, the hosiers were infected, and began to pull down their shop-fronts with frantic recklessness. The mania again died away, and the public began to congratulate themselves on its entire disappearance, when it burst forth with tenfold violence among the publicans, and keepers of 'wine vaults.' From that moment it has spread among them with unprecedented rapidity, exhibiting a concatenation of all the previous symptoms; onward it has rushed to every part of town, knocking down all the old public-houses, and depositing splendid mansions, stone balustrades, rosewood fittings, immense lamps, and illuminated clocks, at the corner of every street.

The extensive scale on which these places are established, and the ostentatious manner in which the business of even the smallest among them is divided into branches, is amusing. A handsome plate of ground glass in one door directs you 'To the Counting-house;' another to the 'Bottle Department; a third to the 'Wholesale Department;' a fourth to 'The Wine Promenade;' and so forth, until we are in daily expectation of meeting with a 'Brandy Bell,' or a 'Whiskey Entrance.' Then, ingenuity is exhausted in devising attractive titles for the different descriptions of gin; and the dram-drinking portion of the community as they gaze upon the gigantic black and white announcements, which are only to be equalled in size by the figures beneath them, are left in a state of pleasing hesitation between 'The Cream of the Valley,' 'The Out and Out,' 'The No Mistake,' 'The Good for Mixing,' 'The real Knock- me-down,' 'The celebrated Butter Gin,' 'The regular Flare-up,' and a dozen other, equally inviting and wholesome LIQUEURS. Although places of this description are to be met with in every second street, they are invariably numerous and splendid in precise proportion to the dirt and poverty of the surrounding neighbourhood. The gin-shops in and near Drury-Lane, Holborn, St. Giles's, Covent-garden, and Clare-market, are the handsomest in London. There is more of filth and squalid misery near those great thorough-fares than in any part of this mighty city.

We will endeavour to sketch the bar of a large gin-shop, and its ordinary customers, for the edification of such of our readers as may not have had opportunities of observing such scenes; and on the chance of finding one well suited to our purpose, we will make for Drury-Lane, through the narrow streets and dirty courts which divide it from Oxford-street, and that classical spot adjoining the brewery at the bottom of Tottenham-court-road, best known to the initiated as the 'Rookery.'

The filthy and miserable appearance of this part of London can hardly be imagined by those (and there are many such) who have not witnessed it. Wretched houses with broken windows patched with rags and paper: every room let out to a different family, and in many instances to two or even three, fruit and 'sweet-stuff' manufacturers in the cellars, barbers and red-herring vendors in the front parlours, cobblers in the back; a bird-fancier in the first floor, three families on the second, starvation in the attics, Irishmen in the passage, a 'musician' in the front kitchen, and a charwoman and five hungry children in the back one, filth everywhere, a gutter before the houses and a drain behind, clothes drying and slops emptying, from the windows; girls of fourteen or fifteen, with matted hair, walking about barefoot, and in white great-coats, almost their only covering; boys of all ages, in coats of all sizes and no coats at all; men and women, in every variety of scanty and dirty apparel, lounging, scolding, drinking, smoking, squabbling, fighting, and swearing.

You turn the corner. What a change! All is light and brilliancy. The hum of many voices issues from that splendid gin-shop which forms the commencement of the two streets opposite; and the gay building with the fantastically ornamented parapet, the illuminated clock, the plate-glass windows surrounded by stucco rosettes, and its profusion of gas-lights in richly-gilt burners, is perfectly dazzling when contrasted with the darkness and dirt we have just left. The interior is even gayer than the exterior. A bar of French-polished mahogany, elegantly carved, extends the whole width of the place; and there are two side-aisles of great casks, painted green and gold, enclosed within a light brass rail, and bearing such inscriptions, as 'Old Tom, 549;' 'Young Tom, 360;' 'Samson, 1421', the figures agreeing, we presume, with 'gallons,' understood. Beyond the bar is a lofty and spacious saloon, full of the same enticing vessels, with a gallery running round it, equally well furnished. On the counter, in addition to the usual spirit apparatus, are two or three little baskets of cakes and biscuits, which are carefully secured at top with wicker-work, to prevent their contents being unlawfully abstracted. Behind it, are two showily-dressed damsels with large necklaces, dispensing the spirits and 'compounds.' They are assisted by the ostensible proprietor of the concern, a stout, coarse fellow in a fur cap, put on very much on one side to give him a knowing air, and to display his sandy whiskers to the best advantage.

The two old washerwomen, who are seated on the little bench to the left of the bar, are rather overcome by the head-dresses and haughty demeanour of the young ladies who officiate. They receive their half-quartern of gin and peppermint, with considerable deference, prefacing a request for 'one of them soft biscuits,' with a 'Jist be good enough, ma'am.' They are quite astonished at the impudent air of the young fellow in a brown coat and bright buttons, who, ushering in his two companions, and walking up to the bar in as careless a manner as if he had been used to green and gold ornaments all his life, winks at one of the young ladies with singular coolness, and calls for a 'kervorten and a three-out- glass,' just as if the place were his own. 'Gin for you, sir?' says the young lady when she has drawn it: carefully looking every way but the right one, to show that the wink had no effect upon her. 'For me, Mary, my dear,' replies the gentleman in brown. 'My name an't Mary as it happens,' says the young girl, rather relaxing as she delivers the change. 'Well, if it an't, it ought to be,' responds the irresistible one; 'all the Marys as ever I see, was handsome gals.' Here the young lady, not precisely remembering how blushes are managed in such cases, abruptly ends the flirtation by addressing the female in the faded feathers who has just entered, and who, after stating explicitly, to prevent any subsequent misunderstanding, that 'this gentleman pays,' calls for 'a glass of port wine and a bit of sugar.'

Those two old men who came in 'just to have a drain,' finished their third quartern a few seconds ago; they have made themselves crying drunk; and the fat comfortable-looking elderly women, who had 'a glass of rum-srub' each, having chimed in with their complaints on the hardness of the times, one of the women has agreed to stand a glass round, jocularly observing that 'grief never mended no broken bones, and as good people's wery scarce, what I says is, make the most on 'em, and that's all about it!' a sentiment which appears to afford unlimited satisfaction to those who have nothing to pay.

It is growing late, and the throng of men, women, and children, who have been constantly going in and out, dwindles down to two or three occasional stragglers, cold, wretched-looking creatures, in the last stage of emaciation and disease. The knot of Irish labourers at the lower end of the place, who have been alternately shaking hands with, and threatening the life of each other, for the last hour, become furious in their disputes, and finding it impossible to silence one man, who is particularly anxious to adjust the difference, they resort to the expedient of knocking him down and jumping on him afterwards. The man in the fur cap, and the potboy rush out; a scene of riot and confusion ensues; half the Irishmen get shut out, and the other half get shut in; the potboy is knocked among the tubs in no time; the landlord hits everybody, and everybody hits the landlord; the barmaids scream; the police come in; the rest is a confused mixture of arms, legs, staves, torn coats, shouting, and struggling. Some of the party are borne off to the station-house, and the remainder slink home to beat their wives for complaining, and kick the children for daring to be hungry.

We have sketched this subject very slightly, not only because our limits compel us to do so, but because, if it were pursued farther, it would be painful and repulsive. Well-disposed gentlemen, and charitable ladies, would alike turn with coldness and disgust from a description of the drunken besotted men, and wretched broken-down miserable women, who form no inconsiderable portion of the frequenters of these haunts; forgetting, in the pleasant consciousness of their own rectitude, the poverty of the one, and the temptation of the other. Gin-drinking is a great vice in England, but wretchedness and dirt are a greater; and until you improve the homes of the poor, or persuade a half-famished wretch not to seek relief in the temporary oblivion of his own misery, with the pittance which, divided among his family, would furnish a morsel of bread for each, gin-shops will increase in number and splendour. If Temperance Societies would suggest an antidote against hunger, filth, and foul air, or could establish dispensaries for the gratuitous distribution of bottles of Lethe-water, gin-palaces would be numbered among the things that were.

The Prisoners' Van

We were passing the corner of Bow-street, on our return from a lounging excursion the other afternoon, when a crowd, assembled round the door of the Police-office, attracted our attention. We turned up the street accordingly. There were thirty or forty people, standing on the pavement and half across the road; and a few stragglers were patiently stationed on the opposite side of the way, all evidently waiting in expectation of some arrival. We waited too, a few minutes, but nothing occurred; so, we turned round to an unshorn, sallow-looking cobbler, who was standing next us with his hands under the bib of his apron, and put the usual question of 'What's the matter?' The cobbler eyed us from head to foot, with superlative contempt, and laconically replied 'Nuffin.'

Now, we were perfectly aware that if two men stop in the street to look at any given object, or even to gaze in the air, two hundred men will be assembled in no time; but, as we knew very well that no crowd of people could by possibility remain in a street for five minutes without getting up a little amusement among themselves, unless they had some absorbing object in view, the natural inquiry next in order was, 'What are all these people waiting here for?' - 'Her Majesty's carriage,' replied the cobbler. This was still more extraordinary. We could not imagine what earthly business Her Majesty's carriage could have at the Public Office, Bow-street. We were beginning to ruminate on the possible causes of such an uncommon appearance, when a general exclamation from all the boys in the crowd of 'Here's the wan!' caused us to raise our heads, and look up the street.

The covered vehicle, in which prisoners are conveyed from the police-offices to the different prisons, was coming along at full speed. It then occurred to us, for the first time, that Her Majesty's carriage was merely another name for the prisoners' van, conferred upon it, not only by reason of the superior gentility of the term, but because the aforesaid van is maintained at Her Majesty's expense: having been originally started for the exclusive accommodation of ladies and gentlemen under the necessity of visiting the various houses of call known by the general denomination of 'Her Majesty's Gaols.'

The van drew up at the office-door, and the people thronged round the steps, just leaving a little alley for the prisoners to pass through. Our friend the cobbler, and the other stragglers, crossed over, and we followed their example. The driver, and another man who had been seated by his side in front of the vehicle, dismounted, and were admitted into the office. The office-door was closed after them, and the crowd were on the tiptoe of expectation.

After a few minutes' delay, the door again opened, and the two first prisoners appeared. They were a couple of girls, of whom the elder could not be more than sixteen, and the younger of whom had certainly not attained her fourteenth year. That they were sisters, was evident, from the resemblance which still subsisted between them, though two additional years of depravity had fixed their brand upon the elder girl's features, as legibly as if a red-hot iron had seared them. They were both gaudily dressed, the younger one especially; and, although there was a strong similarity between them in both respects, which was rendered the more obvious by their being handcuffed together, it is impossible to conceive a greater contrast than the demeanour of the two presented. The younger girl was weeping bitterly, not for display, or in the hope of producing effect, but for very shame: her face was buried in her handkerchief: and her whole manner was but too expressive of bitter and unavailing sorrow.

'How long are you for, Emily?' screamed a red-faced woman in the crowd. 'Six weeks and labour,' replied the elder girl with a flaunting laugh; 'and that's better than the stone jug anyhow; the mill's a deal better than the Sessions, and here's Bella a-going too for the first time. Hold up your head, you chicken,' she continued, boisterously tearing the other girl's handkerchief away; 'Hold up your head, and show 'em your face. I an't jealous, but I'm blessed if I an't game!' - 'That's right, old gal,' exclaimed a man in a paper cap, who, in common with the greater part of the crowd, had been inexpressibly delighted with this little incident. 'Right!' replied the girl; 'ah, to be sure; what's the odds, eh?' - 'Come! In with you,' interrupted the driver. 'Don't you be in a hurry, coachman,' replied the girl, 'and recollect I want to be set down in Cold Bath Fields, large house with a high garden-wall in front; you can't mistake it. Hallo. Bella, where are you going to, you'll pull my precious arm off?' This was addressed to the younger girl, who, in her anxiety to hide herself in the caravan, had ascended the steps first, and forgotten the strain upon the handcuff. 'Come down, and let's show you the way.' And after jerking the miserable girl down with a force which made her stagger on the pavement, she got into the vehicle, and was followed by her wretched companion.

These two girls had been thrown upon London streets, their vices and debauchery, by a sordid and rapacious mother. What the younger girl was then, the elder had been once; and what the elder then was, the younger must soon become. A melancholy prospect, but how surely to be realised; a tragic drama, but how often acted! Turn to the prisons and police offices of London, nay, look into the very streets themselves. These things pass before our eyes, day after day, and hour after hour, they have become such matters of course, that they are utterly disregarded. The progress of these girls in crime will be as rapid as the flight of a pestilence, resembling it too in its baneful influence and wide-spreading infection. Step by step, how many wretched females, within the sphere of every man's observation, have become involved in a career of vice, frightful to contemplate; hopeless at its commencement, loathsome and repulsive in its course; friendless, forlorn, and unpitied, at its miserable conclusion!

There were other prisoners, boys of ten, as hardened in vice as men of fifty, a houseless vagrant, going joyfully to prison as a place of food and shelter, handcuffed to a man whose prospects were ruined, character lost, and family rendered destitute, by his first offence. Our curiosity, however, was satisfied. The first group had left an impression on our mind we would gladly have avoided, and would willingly have effaced.

The crowd dispersed; the vehicle rolled away with its load of guilt and misfortune; and we saw no more of the Prisoners' Van.

The Runaway Couple

The Boots at the Holly Tree Inn was the young man named Cobbs, who blacked the shoes, and ran errands, and waited on the people at the inn; and this is the story that he told, one day.

"Supposing a young gentleman not eight years old was to run away with a fine young woman of seven, would you consider that a queer start? That there is a start as I, the Boots at the Holly Tree Inn, have seen with my own eyes; and I cleaned the shoes they ran away in, and they was so little that I couldn't get my hand into 'em.

"Master Harry Walmers' father, he lived at the Elms, away by Shooter's Hill, six or seven miles from London. He was uncommon proud of Master Harry, as he was his only child; but he didn't spoil him neither. He was a gentleman that had a will of his own, and an eye of his own, and that would be minded. Consequently, though he made quite a companion of the fine bright boy, still he kept the command over him, and the child *was* a child. I was under-gardener there at that time; and one morning Master Harry, he comes to me and says

"'Cobbs, how should you spell Norah, if you was asked?' and then begun cutting it in print, all over the fence.

"He couldn't say he had taken particular notice of children before that; but really it was pretty to see them two mites a-going about the place together, deep in love. And the courage of the boy! Bless your soul, he'd have throwed off his little hat, and tucked up his little sleeves, and gone in at a lion, he would, if they had happened to meet one and she had been frightened of him. One day he stops along, with her, where Boots was hoeing weeds in the gravel, and says speaking up, 'Cobbs,' he says, 'I like you.' 'Do you, sir? I'm proud to hear it.' 'Yes, I do, Cobbs. Why do I like you, do you think, Cobbs?' 'Don't know, Master Harry, I am sure.' 'Because Norah likes you, Cobbs.' 'Indeed, sir? That's very gratifying.' 'Gratifying, Cobbs? It's better than millions of the brightest diamonds to be liked by Norah.' 'Certainly, sir.' 'You're going away, ain't you, Cobbs?' 'Yes, sir.' 'Would you like another situation, Cobbs?' 'Well, sir, I shouldn't object, if it was a good 'un.' 'Then, Cobbs,' says he, 'you shall be our head-gardener when we are married.' And he tucks her, in her little sky-blue mantle, under his arm, and walks away.

"It was better than a picter, and equal to a play, to see them babies with their long, bright, curling hair, their sparkling eyes, and their beautiful light tread, a-rambling about the garden, deep in love. Boots was of opinion that the birds believed they was birds, and kept up with 'em, singing to please 'em. Sometimes, they would creep under the Tulip tree, and would sit there with their arms round one another's necks, and their soft cheeks touching, a-reading about the prince and the dragon, and the good and bad enchanters, and the king's fair daughter. Sometimes he would hear them planning about having a house in a forest, keeping bees and a cow, and living entirely on milk and honey. Once he came upon them by the pond, and heard Master Harry say, 'Adorable Norah, kiss me, and say you love me to distraction, or I'll jump in headforemost.' And Boots made no question he would have done it, if she hadn't done as he asked her.

"'Cobbs,' says Master Harry, one evening, when Cobbs was watering the flowers, 'I am going on a visit, this present mid-summer, to my grandmamma's at York.'

"'Are you, indeed, sir? I hope you'll have a pleasant time. I am going into Yorkshire myself when I leave here.'

"'Are you going to your grandmamma's, Cobbs?'

"'No, sir. I haven't got such a thing.'

"'Not as a grandmamma, Cobbs?'

"'No, sir.'

"The boy looked on at the watering of the flowers for a little while and then said, 'I shall be very glad, indeed, to go, Cobbs, Norah's going.'

"'You'll be all right then, sir,' says Cobbs, 'with your beautiful sweetheart by your side.'

"'Cobbs,' returned the boy, flushing, 'I never let anybody joke about it when I can prevent them.'

"'It wasn't a joke, sir,' says Cobbs, with humility, 'wasn't so meant.'

"'I am glad of that, Cobbs, because I like you! you know, and you're going to live with us, Cobbs.

"'Sir.'

"'What do you think my grandmamma gives me, when I go down there?'

"'I couldn't so much as make a guess, sir.'

"'A Bank of England five-pound note, Cobbs.'[A]

"'Whew!' says Cobbs, 'that's a spanking sum of money, Master Harry.'

"'A person could do a great deal with such a sum of money as that. Couldn't a person, Cobbs?'

"'I believe you, sir!'

"'Cobbs,' said the boy, 'I'll tell you a secret. At Norah's house they have been joking her about me, and pretending to laugh at our being engaged. Pretending to make game of it, Cobbs!'

"'Such, sir,' says Cobbs, 'is the wickedness of human natur'.'

"The boy, looking exactly like his father, stood for a few minutes with his glowing face towards the sunset, and then departed with, 'Good night, Cobbs. I'm going in.'

"I was the Boots at the Holly Tree Inn when one summer afternoon the coach drives up, and out of the coach gets these two children.

"The guard says to our governor, the inn-keeper, 'I don't quite make out these little passengers, but the young gentleman's words was, that they were to be brought here.' The young gentleman gets out; hands his lady out; gives the driver something for himself; says to our governor, 'We're to stop here to-night, please. Sitting-room and two bedrooms will be required. Chops and cherry-pudding for two!' and tucks her, in her little sky-blue mantle, under his arm, and walks into the house much bolder than brass.

"Boots leaves me to judge what the amazement of that establishment was when those two tiny creatures, all alone by themselves, was marched into the parlor, much more so when he, who had seen them without their seeing him, gave the governor his views of the errand they was upon. 'Cobbs,' says the governor, 'if this is so, I must set off myself to York and quiet their friends' minds. In which case you must keep your eye upon 'em, and humor 'em, till I come back. But, before I take these measures, Cobbs, I should wish you to find out from themselves whether your opinions is correct.' 'Sir, to you,' says Cobbs, 'that shall be done directly.'

"So Boots goes up stairs to the parlor, and there he finds Master Harry on an enormous sofa a-drying the eyes of Miss Norah with his pocket-hankecher. Their little legs were entirely off the ground of course, and it really is not possible for Boots to express to me how small them children looked.

"'It's Cobbs! It's Cobbs!' cries Master Harry, and comes running to him, and catching hold of his hand. Miss Norah comes running to him on t'other side, and catching hold of his t'other hand, and they both jump for joy.

"'I see you a-getting out, sir,' says Cobbs. 'I thought it was you. I thought I couldn't be mistaken in your height and figure. What's the object of your journey, sir? Are you going to be married?'

"'We are going to be married, Cobbs, at Gretna Green,' returned the boy. 'We have run away on purpose. Norah has been in rather low spirits, Cobbs; but she'll be happy, now we have found you to be our friend.'

"'Thank you, sir, and thank *you*, miss,' says Cobbs, 'for your good opinion. Did you bring any luggage with you, sir?'

"If I will believe Boots when he gives me his word and honor upon it, the lady had got a parasol, a smelling-bottle, a round and a half of cold buttered toast, eight peppermint drops, and a hair-brush, seemingly a doll's. The gentleman had got about half a dozen yards of string, a knife, three or four sheets of writing-paper folded up surprisingly small, an orange, and a china mug with his name upon it.

"'What may be the exact natur' of your plans, sir?' says Cobbs.

"'To go on,' replied the boy, which the courage of that boy was something wonderful! 'in the morning, and be married to-morrow.'

"'Just so, sir,' says Cobbs. 'Would it meet your views, sir, if I was to go with you?'

"When Cobbs said this, they both jumped for joy again, and cried out, 'Oh, yes, yes, Cobbs! Yes!'

"'Well, sir,' says Cobbs. 'If you will excuse my having the freedom to give an opinion, what I should recommend would be this. I'm acquainted with a pony, sir, which, put in a phaeton that I could borrow, would take you and Mrs. Harry Walmers, Jr. (myself driving, if you agree), to the end of your journey in a very short space of time. I am not altogether sure, sir, that this pony will be at liberty to-morrow, but even if you had to wait over to-morrow for him, it might be worth your while. As to the small account for your board here, sir, in case you was to find yourself running at all short, that don't signify, because I'm a part proprietor of this inn, and it could stand over.'

"Boots tells me that when they clapped their hands and jumped for joy again, and called him, 'Good Cobbs!' and 'Dear Cobbs!' and bent across him to kiss one another in the delight of their trusting hearts, he felt himself the meanest rascal for deceiving 'em that ever was born.

"'Is there anything you want just at present, sir?' says Cobbs, mortally ashamed of himself.

"'We would like some cakes after dinner,' answered Master Harry, folding his arms, putting out one leg, and looking straight at him, 'and two apples, and jam. With dinner, we should like to have toast and water. But Norah has always been accustomed to half a glass of currant wine at dessert. And so have I.'

"'It shall be ordered at the bar, sir,' says Cobbs, and away he went.

"'The way in which the women of that house, without exception, everyone of 'em, married and single, took to that boy when they heard the story, Boots considers surprising. It was as much as he could do to keep 'em from dashing into the room and kissing him. They climbed up all sorts of places, at the risk of their lives, to look at him through a pane of glass. They were seven deep at the key-hole. They were out of their minds about him and his bold spirit.

"In the evening Boots went into the room, to see how the runaway couple was getting on. The gentleman was on the window-seat, supporting the lady in his arms. She had tears upon her face, and was lying, very tired and half-asleep, with her head upon his shoulder.

"'Mrs. Harry Walmers, Jr., tired, sir?' says Cobbs.

"'Yes, she is tired, Cobbs; but she is not used to be away from home, and she has been in low spirits again. Cobbs, do you think you could bring a biffin, please?'

"'I ask your pardon, sir,' says Cobbs. 'What was it you'

"'I think a Norfolk biffin[B] would rouse her, Cobbs. She is very fond of them.'

"Boots withdrew in search of the required restorative, and, when he brought it in, the gentleman handed it to the lady, and fed her with a spoon, and took a little himself. The lady being heavy with sleep, and rather cross. 'What should you think, sir,' says Cobbs, 'of a chamber candlestick?' The gentleman approved; the chambermaid went first, up the great staircase; the lady, in her sky-blue mantle, followed, gallantly led by the gentleman; the gentleman kissed her at the door, and retired to his own room, where Boots softly locked him up.

"Boots couldn't but feel what a base deceiver he was when they asked him at breakfast (they had ordered sweet milk-and-water, and toast and currant jelly, overnight) about the pony. It really was as much as he could do, he don't mind confessing to me, to look them two young things in the face, and think how wicked he had grown up to be. Howsomever, he went on a-lying like a Trojan, about the pony. He told 'em it did so unfortunately happen that the pony was half-clipped, you see, and that he couldn't be taken out in that state for fear that it should strike to his inside. But that he'd be finished clipping in the course of the day, and that to-morrow morning at eight o'clock the phaeton would be ready. Boots' view of the whole case, looking back upon it in my room, is, that Mrs. Harry Walmers, Jr., was beginning to give in. She hadn't had her hair curled when she went to bed, and she didn't seem quite up to brushing it herself, and it's getting in her eyes put her out. But nothing put out Master Harry. He sat behind his breakfast cup, a-tearing away at the jelly, as if he had been his own father.

"After breakfast Boots is inclined to think that they drawed soldiers, at least, he knows that many such was found in the fireplace, all on horseback. In the course of the morning Master Harry rang the bell, it was surprising how that there boy did carry on and said in a sprightly way, 'Cobbs, is there any good walks in this neighborhood?'

"'Yes, sir,' says Cobbs. 'There's Love Lane.'

"'Get out with you, Cobbs!' that was that there boy's expression, 'you're joking.'

"'Begging your pardon, sir,' says Cobbs, 'there really is Love Lane. And a pleasant walk it is, and proud I shall be to show it to yourself and Mrs. Harry Walmers, Jr.'

"'Norah, dear,' said Master Harry, 'this is curious. We really ought to see Love Lane. Put on your bonnet, my sweetest darling, and we will go there with Cobbs.'

"Boots leaves me to judge what a beast he felt himself to be, when that young pair told him, as they all three jogged along together, that they had made up their minds to give him two thousand guineas a year as head-gardener, on account of his being so true a friend to 'em. Boots could have wished at the moment that the earth would have opened and swallowed him up; he felt so mean with their beaming eyes a-looking at him, and believing him. Well, sir, he turned the conversation as well as he could, and he took 'em down Love Lane to the water-meadows, and there Master Harry would have drowned himself in half a moment more, a-getting out a water-lily for her, but nothing frightened that boy. Well, sir, they was tired out. All being so new and strange to 'em, they was tired as tired could be. And they laid down on a bank of daisies, like the children in the wood, leastways meadows, and fell asleep.

"Well, sir, they woke up at last, and then one thing was getting pretty clear to Boots, namely, that Mrs. Harry Walmers', Jr., temper was on the move. When Master Harry took her round the waist she said he 'teased her so,' and when he says, 'Norah, my young May Moon, your Harry tease you?' she tells him, 'Yes; and I want to go home!'

"However, Master Harry he kept up, and his noble heart was as fond as ever. Mrs. Walmers turned very sleepy about dusk and began to cry. Therefore, Mrs. Walmers went off to bed as per yesterday; and Master Harry ditto repeated.

"About eleven or twelve at night comes back the inn-keeper in a chaise, along with Mr. Walmers and an elderly lady. Mr. Walmers looks amused and very serious, both at once, and says to our missis, 'We are very much indebted to you, ma'am, for your kind care of our little children, which we can never sufficiently acknowledge. Pray, ma'am where is my boy?' Our missis says, 'Cobbs has the dear children in charge, sir. Cobbs, show forty!' Then he says to Cobbs, 'Ah, Cobbs! I am glad to see *you*. I understand you was here!' And Cobbs says, 'Yes, sir. Your most obedient, sir.'

"I may be surprised to hear Boots say it, perhaps, but Boots assures me that his heart beat like a hammer, going up-stairs. 'I beg your pardon, sir,' says he, while unlocking the door; 'I hope you are not angry with Master Harry. For Master Harry is a fine boy, sir, and will do you credit and honor.' And Boots signifies to me that if the fine boy's father had contradicted him in the daring state of mind in which he then was, he thinks he should have 'fetched him a crack,' and taken the consequences.

"But Mr. Walmers only says, 'No, Cobbs. No, my good fellow. Thank you!' And the door being open, goes in.

"Boots goes in too, holding the light, and he sees Mr. Walmers go up to the bedside, bend gently down, and kiss the little sleeping face. Then he stands looking at it for a minute, looking wonderfully like it; and then he gently shakes the little shoulder.

"'Harry, my dear boy! Harry!'

"Master Harry starts up and looks at him. Looks at Cobbs, too. Such is the honor of that mite that he looks at Cobbs to see whether he has brought him into trouble.

"'I am not angry, my child. I only want you to dress yourself and come home.'

"'Yes, pa.'

"Master Harry dresses himself quickly. His breast begins to swell when he has nearly finished, and it swells more and more as he stands a-looking at his father; his father standing a-looking at him, the quiet image of him.

"'Please may I', the spirit of that little creatur', and the way he kept his rising tears down! 'Please, dear pa, may I, kiss Norah before I go?'

"'You may, my child.'

"So he takes Master Harry in his hand, and Boots leads the way with the candle, and they come to that other bedroom; where the elderly lady is seated by the bed, and poor little Mrs. Harry Walmers, Jr., is fast asleep. There the father lifts the child up to the pillow, and he lays his little face down for an instant by the little warm face of poor unconscious little Mrs. Harry Walmers, Jr., and gently draws it to him, a sight so touching to the chambermaids who are peeping through the door that one of them calls out, 'It's a shame to part 'em!' But this chambermaid was always, as Boots informs me, a soft-hearted one. Not that there was any harm in that girl. Far from it."

FOOTNOTES:

[A] For the benefit of some of our young readers, it may be well to explain that this is about the same as a bill of twenty-five dollars would be in America.

[B] A biffin is a red apple, growing near Norfolk, and generally eaten after having been baked.

Shabby-Genteel People

There are certain descriptions of people who, oddly enough, appear to appertain exclusively to the metropolis. You meet them, every day, in the streets of London, but no one ever encounters them elsewhere; they seem indigenous to the soil, and to belong as exclusively to London as its own smoke, or the dingy bricks and mortar. We could illustrate the remark by a variety of examples, but, in our present sketch, we will only advert to one class as a specimen, that class which is so aptly and expressively designated as 'shabby-genteel.'

Now, shabby people, God knows, may be found anywhere, and genteel people are not articles of greater scarcity out of London than in it; but this compound of the two, this shabby-gentility, is as purely local as the statue at Charing-cross, or the pump at Aldgate. It is worthy of remark, too, that only men are shabby- genteel; a woman is always either dirty and slovenly in the extreme, or neat and respectable, however poverty-stricken in appearance. A very poor man, 'who has seen better days,' as the phrase goes, is a strange compound of dirty-slovenliness and wretched attempts at faded smartness.

We will endeavour to explain our conception of the term which forms the title of this paper. If you meet a man, lounging up Drury- Lane, or leaning with his back against a post in Long-acre, with his hands in the pockets of a pair of drab trousers plentifully besprinkled with grease-spots: the trousers made very full over the boots, and ornamented with two cords down the outside of each leg, wearing, also, what has been a brown coat with bright buttons, and a hat very much pinched up at the side, cocked over his right eye, don't pity him. He is not shabby-genteel. The 'harmonic meetings' at some fourth-rate public-house, or the purlieus of a private theatre, are his chosen haunts; he entertains a rooted antipathy to any kind of work, and is on familiar terms with several pantomime men at the large houses. But, if you see hurrying along a by-street, keeping as close as he can to the area- railings, a man of about forty or fifty, clad in an old rusty suit of threadbare black cloth which shines with constant wear as if it had been bees-waxed, the trousers tightly strapped down, partly for the look of the thing and partly to keep his old shoes from slipping off at the heels, if you observe, too, that his yellowish-white neckerchief is carefully pinned up, to conceal the tattered garment underneath, and that his hands are encased in the remains of an old pair of beaver gloves, you may set him down as a shabby-genteel man. A glance at that depressed face, and timorous air of conscious poverty, will make your heart ache, always supposing that you are neither a philosopher nor a political economist.

We were once haunted by a shabby-genteel man; he was bodily present to our senses all day, and he was in our mind's eye all night. The man of whom Sir Walter Scott speaks in his Demonology, did not suffer half the persecution from his imaginary gentleman-usher in black velvet, that we sustained from our friend in quondam black cloth. He first attracted our notice, by sitting opposite to us in the reading-room at the British Museum; and what made the man more remarkable was, that he always had before him a couple of shabby- genteel books, two old dog's-eared folios, in mouldy worm-eaten covers, which had once been smart. He was in his chair, every morning, just as the clock struck ten; he was always the last to leave the room in the afternoon; and when he did, he quitted it with the air of a man who knew not where else to go, for warmth and quiet. There he used to sit all day, as close to the table as possible, in order to conceal the lack of buttons on his coat: with his old hat carefully deposited at his feet, where he evidently flattered himself it escaped observation.

About two o'clock, you would see him munching a French roll or a penny loaf; not taking it boldly out of his pocket at once, like a man who knew he was only making a lunch; but breaking off little bits in his pocket, and eating them by stealth. He knew too well it was his dinner.

When we first saw this poor object, we thought it quite impossible that his attire could ever become worse. We even went so far, as to speculate on the possibility of his shortly appearing in a decent second-hand suit. We knew nothing about the matter; he grew more and more shabby-genteel every day. The buttons dropped off his waistcoat, one by one; then, he buttoned his coat; and when one side of the coat was reduced to the same condition as the waistcoat, he buttoned it over, on the other side. He looked somewhat better at the beginning of the week than at the conclusion, because the neckerchief, though yellow, was not quite so dingy; and, in the midst of all this wretchedness, he never appeared without gloves and straps. He remained in this state for a week or two. At length, one of the buttons on the back of the coat fell off, and then the man himself disappeared, and we thought he was dead.

We were sitting at the same table about a week after his disappearance, and as our eyes rested on his vacant chair, we insensibly fell into a train of meditation on the subject of his retirement from public life. We were wondering whether he had hung himself, or thrown himself off a bridge, whether he really was dead or had only been arrested, when our conjectures were suddenly set at rest by the entry of the man himself. He had undergone some strange metamorphosis, and walked up the centre of the room with an air which showed he was fully conscious of the improvement in his appearance. It was very odd. His clothes were a fine, deep, glossy black; and yet they looked like the same suit; nay, there were the very darns with which old acquaintance had made us familiar. The hat, too, nobody could mistake the shape of that hat, with its high crown gradually increasing in circumference towards the top. Long service had imparted to it a reddish-brown tint; but, now, it was as black as the coat. The truth flashed suddenly upon us, they had been 'revived.' It is a deceitful liquid that black and blue reviver; we have watched its effects on many a shabby-genteel man. It betrays its victims into a temporary assumption of importance: possibly into the purchase of a new pair of gloves, or a cheap stock, or some other trifling article of dress. It elevates their spirits for a week, only to depress them, if possible, below their original level. It was so in this case; the transient dignity of the unhappy man decreased, in exact proportion as the 'reviver' wore off. The knees of the unmentionables, and the elbows of the coat, and the seams generally, soon began to get alarmingly white. The hat was once more deposited under the table, and its owner crept into his seat as quietly as ever.

There was a week of incessant small rain and mist. At its expiration the 'reviver' had entirely vanished, and the shabby- genteel man never afterwards attempted to effect any improvement in his outward appearance.

It would be difficult to name any particular part of town as the principal resort of shabby-genteel men. We have met a great many persons of this description in the neighbourhood of the inns of court. They may be met with, in Holborn, between eight and ten any morning; and whoever has the curiosity to enter the Insolvent Debtors' Court will observe, both among spectators and practitioners, a great variety of them. We never went on 'Change, by any chance, without seeing some shabby-genteel men, and we have often wondered what earthly business they can have there. They will sit there, for hours, leaning on great, dropsical, mildewed umbrellas, or eating Abernethy biscuits. Nobody speaks to them, nor they to any one. On consideration, we remember to have occasionally seen two shabby-genteel men conversing together on 'Change, but our experience assures us that this is an uncommon circumstance, occasioned by the offer of a pinch of snuff, or some such civility.

It would be a task of equal difficulty, either to assign any particular spot for the residence of these beings, or to endeavour to enumerate their general occupations. We were never engaged in business with more than one shabby-genteel man; and he was a drunken engraver, and lived in a damp back-parlour in a new row of houses at Camden-town, half street, half brick-field, somewhere near the canal. A shabby-genteel man may have no occupation, or he may be a corn agent, or a coal agent, or a wine merchant, or a collector of debts, or a broker's assistant, or a broken-down attorney. He may be a clerk of the lowest description, or a contributor to the press of the same grade. Whether our readers have noticed these men, in their walks, as often as we have, we know not; this we know, that the miserably poor man (no matter whether he owes his distresses to his own conduct, or that of others) who feels his poverty and vainly strives to conceal it, is one of the most pitiable objects in human nature. Such objects, with few exceptions, are shabby-genteel people.

Bill-Sticking

If I had an enemy whom I hated - which Heaven forbid! - and if I knew of something which sat heavy on his conscience, I think I would introduce that something into a Posting-Bill, and place a large impression in the hands of an active sticker. I can scarcely imagine a more terrible revenge. I should haunt him, by this means, night and day. I do not mean to say that I would publish his secret, in red letters two feet high, for all the town to read: I would darkly refer to it. It should be between him, and me, and the Posting-Bill. Say, for example, that, at a certain period of his life, my enemy had surreptitiously possessed himself of a key. I would then embark my capital in the lock business, and conduct that business on the advertising principle. In all my placards and advertisements, I would throw up the line SECRET KEYS. Thus, if my enemy passed an uninhabited house, he would see his conscience glaring down on him from the parapets, and peeping up at him from the cellars. If he took a dead wall in his walk, it would be alive with reproaches. If he sought refuge in an omnibus, the panels thereof would become Belshazzar's palace to him. If he took boat, in a wild endeavour to escape, he would see the fatal words lurking under the arches of the bridges over the Thames. If he walked the streets with downcast eyes, he would recoil from the very stones of the pavement, made eloquent by lamp-black lithograph. If he drove or rode, his way would be blocked up by enormous vans, each proclaiming the same words over and over again from its whole extent of surface. Until, having gradually grown thinner and paler, and having at last totally rejected food, he would miserably perish, and I should be revenged. This conclusion I should, no doubt, celebrate by laughing a hoarse laugh in three syllables, and folding my arms tight upon my chest agreeably to most of the examples of glutted animosity that I have had an opportunity of observing in connexion with the Drama - which, by-the-by, as involving a good deal of noise, appears to me to be occasionally confounded with the Drummer.

The foregoing reflections presented themselves to my mind, the other day, as I contemplated (being newly come to London from the East Riding of Yorkshire, on a house-hunting expedition for next May), an old warehouse which rotting paste and rotting paper had brought down to the condition of an old cheese. It would have been impossible to say, on the most conscientious survey, how much of its front was brick and mortar, and how much decaying and decayed plaster. It was so thickly encrusted with fragments of bills, that no ship's keel after a long voyage could be half so foul. All traces of the broken windows were billed out, the doors were billed across, the water-spout was billed over. The building was shored up to prevent its tumbling into the street; and the very beams erected against it were less wood than paste and paper, they had been so continually posted and reposted. The forlorn dregs of old posters so encumbered this wreck, that there was no hold for new posters, and the stickers had abandoned the place in despair, except one enterprising man who had hoisted the last masquerade to a clear spot near the level of the stack of chimneys where it waved and drooped like a shattered flag. Below the rusty cellar-grating, crumpled remnants of old bills torn down, rotted away in wasting heaps of fallen leaves. Here and there, some of the thick rind of the house had peeled off in strips, and fluttered heavily down, littering the street; but, still, below these rents and gashes, layers of decomposing posters showed themselves, as if they were interminable. I thought the building could never even be pulled down, but in one adhesive heap of rottenness and poster. As to getting in - I don't believe that if the Sleeping Beauty and her Court had been so billed up, the young Prince could have done it.

Knowing all the posters that were yet legible, intimately, and pondering on their ubiquitous nature, I was led into the reflections with which I began this paper, by considering what an awful thing it would be, ever to have wronged - say M. JULLIEN for example - and to have his avenging name in characters of fire incessantly before my eyes. Or to have injured MADAME TUSSAUD, and undergo a similar retribution. Has any man a self-reproachful thought associated with pills, or ointment? What an avenging spirit to that man is PROFESSOR HOLLOWAY! Have I sinned in oil? CABBURN pursues me. Have I a dark remembrance associated with any gentlemanly garments, bespoke or ready made? MOSES and SON are on my track. Did I ever aim a blow at a defenceless fellow-creature's head? That head eternally being measured for a wig, or that worse head which was bald before it used the balsam, and hirsute afterwards - enforcing the benevolent moral, 'Better to be bald as a Dutch cheese than come to this,' - undoes me. Have I no sore places in my mind which MECHI touches - which NICOLL probes - which no registered article whatever lacerates? Does no discordant note within me thrill responsive to mysterious watchwords, as 'Revalenta Arabica,' or 'Number One St. Paul's Churchyard'? Then may I enjoy life, and be happy.

Lifting up my eyes, as I was musing to this effect, I beheld advancing towards me (I was then on Cornhill, near to the Royal Exchange), a solemn procession of three advertising vans, of first- class dimensions, each drawn by a very little horse. As the cavalcade approached, I was at a loss to reconcile the careless deportment of the drivers of these vehicles, with the terrific announcements they conducted through the city, which being a summary of the contents of a Sunday newspaper, were of the most thrilling kind. Robbery, fire, murder, and the ruin of the United Kingdom - each discharged in a line by itself, like a separate broad-side of red-hot shot - were among the least of the warnings addressed to an unthinking people. Yet, the Ministers of Fate who drove the awful cars, leaned forward with their arms upon their knees in a state of extreme lassitude, for want of any subject of interest. The first man, whose hair I might naturally have expected to see standing on end, scratched his head - one of the smoothest I ever beheld - with profound indifference. The second whistled. The third yawned.

Pausing to dwell upon this apathy, it appeared to me, as the fatal cars came by me, that I descried in the second car, through the portal in which the charioteer was seated, a figure stretched upon the floor. At the same time, I thought I smelt tobacco. The latter impression passed quickly from me; the former remained. Curious to know whether this prostrate figure was the one impressible man of the whole capital who had been stricken insensible by the terrors revealed to him, and whose form had been placed in the car by the charioteer, from motives of humanity, I followed the procession. It turned into Leadenhall-market, and halted at a public-house. Each driver dismounted. I then distinctly heard, proceeding from the second car, where I had dimly seen the prostrate form, the words:

'And a pipe!'

The driver entering the public-house with his fellows, apparently for purposes of refreshment, I could not refrain from mounting on the shaft of the second vehicle, and looking in at the portal. I then beheld, reclining on his back upon the floor, on a kind of mattress or divan, a little man in a shooting-coat. The exclamation 'Dear me' which irresistibly escaped my lips caused him to sit upright, and survey me. I found him to be a good-looking little man of about fifty, with a shining face, a tight head, a bright eye, a moist wink, a quick speech, and a ready air. He had something of a sporting way with him.

He looked at me, and I looked at him, until the driver displaced me by handing in a pint of beer, a pipe, and what I understand is called 'a screw' of tobacco - an object which has the appearance of a curl-paper taken off the barmaid's head, with the curl in it.

'I beg your pardon,' said I, when the removed person of the driver again admitted of my presenting my face at the portal. 'But - excuse my curiosity, which I inherit from my mother - do you live here?'

'That's good, too!' returned the little man, composedly laying aside a pipe he had smoked out, and filling the pipe just brought to him.

'Oh, you DON'T live here then?' said I.

He shook his head, as he calmly lighted his pipe by means of a German tinder-box, and replied, 'This is my carriage. When things are flat, I take a ride sometimes, and enjoy myself. I am the inventor of these wans.'

His pipe was now alight. He drank his beer all at once, and he smoked and he smiled at me.

'It was a great idea!' said I.

'Not so bad,' returned the little man, with the modesty of merit.

'Might I be permitted to inscribe your name upon the tablets of my memory?' I asked.

'There's not much odds in the name,' returned the little man, ' - no name particular - I am the King of the Bill-Stickers.'

'Good gracious!' said I.

The monarch informed me, with a smile, that he had never been crowned or installed with any public ceremonies, but that he was peaceably acknowledged as King of the Bill-Stickers in right of being the oldest and most respected member of 'the old school of bill-sticking.' He likewise gave me to understand that there was a Lord Mayor of the Bill-Stickers, whose genius was chiefly exercised within the limits of the city. He made some allusion, also, to an inferior potentate, called 'Turkey-legs;' but I did not understand that this gentleman was invested with much power. I rather inferred that he derived his title from some peculiarity of gait, and that it was of an honorary character.

'My father,' pursued the King of the Bill-Stickers, 'was Engineer, Beadle, and Bill-Sticker to the parish of St. Andrew's, Holborn, in the year one thousand seven hundred and eighty. My father stuck bills at the time of the riots of London.'

'You must be acquainted with the whole subject of bill-sticking, from that time to the present!' said I.

'Pretty well so,' was the answer.

'Excuse me,' said I; 'but I am a sort of collector - '

"Not Income-tax?' cried His Majesty, hastily removing his pipe from his lips.

'No, no,' said I.

'Water-rate?' said His Majesty.

'No, no,' I returned.

'Gas? Assessed? Sewers?' said His Majesty.

'You misunderstand me,' I replied, soothingly. 'Not that sort of collector at all: a collector of facts.'

'Oh, if it's only facts,' cried the King of the Bill-Stickers, recovering his good-humour, and banishing the great mistrust that had suddenly fallen upon him, 'come in and welcome! If it had been income, or winders, I think I should have pitched you out of the wan, upon my soul!'

Readily complying with the invitation, I squeezed myself in at the small aperture. His Majesty, graciously handing me a little three- legged stool on which I took my seat in a corner, inquired if I smoked.

'I do; - that is, I can,' I answered.

'Pipe and a screw!' said His Majesty to the attendant charioteer. 'Do you prefer a dry smoke, or do you moisten it?'

As unmitigated tobacco produces most disturbing effects upon my system (indeed, if I had perfect moral courage, I doubt if I should smoke at all, under any circumstances), I advocated moisture, and begged the Sovereign of the Bill-Stickers to name his usual liquor, and to concede to me the privilege of paying for it. After some delicate reluctance on his part, we were provided, through the instrumentality of the attendant charioteer, with a can of cold rum-and-water, flavoured with sugar and lemon. We were also furnished with a tumbler, and I was provided with a pipe. His Majesty, then observing that we might combine business with conversation, gave the word for the car to proceed; and, to my great delight, we jogged away at a foot pace.

I say to my great delight, because I am very fond of novelty, and it was a new sensation to be jolting through the tumult of the city in that secluded Temple, partly open to the sky, surrounded by the roar without, and seeing nothing but the clouds. Occasionally, blows from whips fell heavily on the Temple's walls, when by stopping up the road longer than usual, we irritated carters and coachmen to madness; but they fell harmless upon us within and disturbed not the serenity of our peaceful retreat. As I looked upward, I felt, I should imagine, like the Astronomer Royal. I was enchanted by the contrast between the freezing nature of our external mission on the blood of the populace, and the perfect composure reigning within those sacred precincts: where His Majesty, reclining easily on his left arm, smoked his pipe and drank his rum-and-water from his own side of the tumbler, which stood impartially between us. As I looked down from the clouds and caught his royal eye, he understood my reflections. 'I have an idea,' he observed, with an upward glance, 'of training scarlet runners across in the season, - making a arbour of it, - and sometimes taking tea in the same, according to the song.'

I nodded approval.

'And here you repose and think?' said I.

'And think,' said he, 'of posters - walls - and hoardings.'

We were both silent, contemplating the vastness of the subject. I remembered a surprising fancy of dear THOMAS HOOD'S, and wondered whether this monarch ever sighed to repair to the great wall of China, and stick bills all over it.

'And so,' said he, rousing himself, 'it's facts as you collect?'

'Facts,' said I.

'The facts of bill-sticking,' pursued His Majesty, in a benignant manner, 'as known to myself, air as following. When my father was Engineer, Beadle, and Bill-Sticker to the parish of St. Andrew's, Holborn, he employed women to post bills for him. He employed women to post bills at the time of the riots of London. He died at the age of seventy-five year, and was buried by the murdered Eliza Grimwood, over in the Waterloo Road.'

As this was somewhat in the nature of a royal speech, I listened with deference and silently. His Majesty, taking a scroll from his pocket, proceeded, with great distinctness, to pour out the following flood of information:-

'"The bills being at that period mostly proclamations and declarations, and which were only a demy size, the manner of posting the bills (as they did not use brushes) was by means of a piece of wood which they called a 'dabber.' Thus things continued till such time as the State Lottery was passed, and then the printers began to print larger bills, and men were employed instead of women, as the State Lottery Commissioners then began to send men all over England to post bills, and would keep them out for six or eight months at a time, and they were called by the London bill- stickers 'TRAMPERS,' their wages at the time being ten shillings per day, besides expenses. They used sometimes to be stationed in large towns for five or six months together, distributing the schemes to all the houses in the town. And then there were more caricature wood-block engravings for posting-bills than there are at the present time, the principal printers, at that time, of posting-bills being Messrs.

Evans and Ruffy, of Budge Row; Thoroughgood and Whiting, of the present day; and Messrs. Gye and Balne, Gracechurch Street, City. The largest bills printed at that period were a two-sheet double crown; and when they commenced printing four-sheet bills, two bill-stickers would work together. They had no settled wages per week, but had a fixed price for their work, and the London bill-stickers, during a lottery week, have been known to earn, each, eight or nine pounds per week, till the day of drawing; likewise the men who carried boards in the street used to have one pound per week, and the bill-stickers at that time would not allow any one to wilfully cover or destroy their bills, as they had a society amongst themselves, and very frequently dined together at some public-house where they used to go of an evening to have their work delivered untoe 'em."'

All this His Majesty delivered in a gallant manner; posting it, as it were, before me, in a great proclamation. I took advantage of the pause he now made, to inquire what a 'two-sheet double crown' might express?

'A two-sheet double crown,' replied the King, 'is a bill thirty- nine inches wide by thirty inches high.'

'Is it possible,' said I, my mind reverting to the gigantic admonitions we were then displaying to the multitude - which were as infants to some of the posting-bills on the rotten old warehouse - 'that some few years ago the largest bill was no larger than that?'

'The fact,' returned the King, 'is undoubtedly so.' Here he instantly rushed again into the scroll.

'"Since the abolishing of the State Lottery all that good feeling has gone, and nothing but jealousy exists, through the rivalry of each other. Several bill-sticking companies have started, but have failed. The first party that started a company was twelve year ago; but what was left of the old school and their dependants joined together and opposed them. And for some time we were quiet again, till a printer of Hatton Garden formed a company by hiring the sides of houses; but he was not supported by the public, and he left his wooden frames fixed up for rent. The last company that started, took advantage of the New Police Act, and hired of Messrs. Grissell and Peto the hoarding of Trafalgar Square, and established a bill-sticking office in Cursitor Street, Chancery Lane, and engaged some of the new bill-stickers to do their work, and for a time got the half of all our work, and with such spirit did they carry on their opposition towards us, that they used to give us in charge before the magistrate, and get us fined; but they found it so expensive, that they could not keep it up, for they were always employing a lot of ruffians from the Seven Dials to come and fight us; and on one occasion the old bill-stickers went to Trafalgar Square to attempt to post bills, when they were given in custody by the watchman in their employ, and fined at Queen Square five pounds, as they would not allow any of us to speak in the office; but when they were gone, we had an interview with the magistrate, who mitigated the fine to fifteen shillings. During the time the men were waiting for the fine, this company started off to a public-house that we were in the habit of using, and waited for us coming back, where a fighting scene took place that beggars description. Shortly after this, the principal one day came and shook hands with us, and acknowledged that he had broken up the company, and that he himself had lost five hundred pound in trying to overthrow us. We then took possession of the hoarding in Trafalgar Square; but Messrs. Grissell and Peto would not allow us to post our bills on the said hoarding without paying them - and from first to last we paid upwards of two hundred pounds for that hoarding, and likewise the hoarding of the Reform Club-house, Pall Mall."'

His Majesty, being now completely out of breath, laid down his scroll (which he appeared to have finished), puffed at his pipe, and took some rum-and-water. I embraced the opportunity of asking how many divisions the art and mystery of bill-sticking comprised? He replied, three - auctioneers' bill-sticking, theatrical bill-sticking, general bill-sticking.

'The auctioneers' porters,' said the King, 'who do their bill- sticking, are mostly respectable and intelligent, and generally well paid for their work, whether in town or country. The price paid by the principal auctioneers for country work is nine shillings per day; that is, seven shillings for day's work, one shilling for lodging, and one for paste. Town work is five shillings a day, including paste.'

'Town work must be rather hot work,' said I, 'if there be many of those fighting scenes that beggar description, among the bill- stickers?'

'Well,' replied the King, 'I an't a stranger, I assure you, to black eyes; a bill-sticker ought to know how to handle his fists a bit. As to that row I have mentioned, that grew out of competition, conducted in an uncompromising spirit. Besides a man in a horse-and-shay continually following us about, the company had a watchman on duty, night and day, to prevent us sticking bills upon the hoarding in Trafalgar Square. We went there, early one morning, to stick bills and to black-wash their bills if we were interfered with. We WERE interfered with, and I gave the word for laying on the wash. It WAS laid on - pretty brisk - and we were all taken to Queen Square: but they couldn't fine ME. I knew that,' - with a bright smile - 'I'd only give directions - I was only the General.' Charmed with this monarch's affability, I inquired if he had ever hired a hoarding himself.

'Hired a large one,' he replied, 'opposite the Lyceum Theatre, when the buildings was there. Paid thirty pound for it; let out places on it, and called it "The External Paper-Hanging Station." But it didn't answer. Ah!' said His Majesty thoughtfully, as he filled the glass, 'Bill-stickers have a deal to contend with. The bill- sticking clause was got into the Police Act by a member of Parliament that employed me at his election. The clause is pretty stiff respecting where bills go; but HE didn't mind where HIS bills went. It was all right enough, so long as they was HIS bills!'

Fearful that I observed a shadow of misanthropy on the King's cheerful face, I asked whose ingenious invention that was, which I greatly admired, of sticking bills under the arches of the bridges.

'Mine!' said His Majesty. 'I was the first that ever stuck a bill under a bridge! Imitators soon rose up, of course. - When don't they? But they stuck 'em at low-water, and the tide came and swept the bills clean away. I knew that!' The King laughed.

'What may be the name of that instrument, like an immense fishing- rod,' I inquired, 'with which bills are posted on high places?'

'The joints,' returned His Majesty. 'Now, we use the joints where formerly we used ladders - as they do still in country places. Once, when Madame' (Vestris, understood) 'was playing in Liverpool, another bill-sticker and me were at it together on the wall outside the Clarence Dock - me with the joints - him on a ladder. Lord! I had my bill up, right over his head, yards above him, ladder and all, while he was crawling to his work. The people going in and out of the docks, stood and laughed! - It's about thirty years since the joints come in.'

'Are there any bill-stickers who can't read?' I took the liberty of inquiring.

'Some,' said the King. 'But they know which is the right side up'ards of their work. They keep it as it's given out to 'em. I have seen a bill or so stuck wrong side up'ards. But it's very rare.'

Our discourse sustained some interruption at this point, by the procession of cars occasioning a stoppage of about three-quarters of a mile in length, as nearly as I could judge. His Majesty, however, entreating me not to be discomposed by the contingent uproar, smoked with great placidity, and surveyed the firmament.

When we were again in motion, I begged to be informed what was the largest poster His Majesty had ever seen. The King replied, 'A thirty-six sheet poster.' I gathered, also, that there were about a hundred and fifty bill-stickers in London, and that His Majesty considered an average hand equal to the posting of one hundred bills (single sheets) in a day. The King was of opinion, that, although posters had much increased in size, they had not increased in number; as the abolition of the State Lotteries had occasioned a great falling off, especially in the country. Over and above which change, I bethought myself that the custom of advertising in newspapers had greatly increased. The completion of many London improvements, as Trafalgar Square (I particularly observed the singularity of His Majesty's calling THAT an improvement), the Royal Exchange, &c., had of late years reduced the number of advantageous posting-places. Bill-Stickers at present rather confine themselves to districts, than to particular descriptions of work. One man would strike over Whitechapel, another would take round Houndsditch, Shoreditch, and the City Road; one (the King said) would stick to the Surrey side; another would make a beat of the West-end.

His Majesty remarked, with some approach to severity, on the neglect of delicacy and taste, gradually introduced into the trade by the new school: a profligate and inferior race of impostors who took jobs at almost any price, to the detriment of the old school, and the confusion of their own misguided employers. He considered that the trade was overdone with competition, and observed speaking of his subjects, 'There are too many of 'em.' He believed, still, that things were a little better than they had been; adducing, as a proof, the fact that particular posting places were now reserved, by common consent, for particular posters; those places, however, must be regularly occupied by those posters, or, they lapsed and fell into other hands. It was of no use giving a man a Drury Lane bill this week and not next. Where was it to go? He was of opinion that going to the expense of putting up your own board on which your sticker could display your own bills, was the only complete way of posting yourself at the present time; but, even to effect this, on payment of a shilling a week to the keepers of steamboat piers and other such places, you must be able, besides, to give orders for theatres and public exhibitions, or you would be sure to be cut out by somebody. His Majesty regarded the passion for orders, as one of the most unappeasable appetites of human nature. If there were a building, or if there were repairs, going on, anywhere, you could generally stand something and make it right with the foreman of the works; but, orders would be expected from you, and the man who could give the most orders was the man who would come off best. There was this other objectionable point, in orders, that workmen sold them for drink, and often sold them to persons who were likewise troubled with the weakness of thirst: which led (His Majesty said) to the presentation of your orders at Theatre doors, by individuals who were 'too shakery' to derive intellectual profit from the entertainments, and who brought a scandal on you. Finally, His Majesty said that you could hardly put too little in a poster; what you wanted, was, two or three good catch-lines for the eye to rest on - then, leave it alone - and there you were!

These are the minutes of my conversation with His Majesty, as I noted them down shortly afterwards. I am not aware that I have been betrayed into any alteration or suppression. The manner of the King was frank in the extreme; and he seemed to me to avoid, at once that slight tendency to repetition which may have been observed in the conversation of His Majesty King George the Third, and - that slight under-current of egotism which the curious observer may perhaps detect in the conversation of Napoleon Bonaparte.

I must do the King the justice to say that it was I, and not he, who closed the dialogue. At this juncture, I became the subject of a remarkable optical delusion; the legs of my stool appeared to me to double up; the car to spin round and round with great violence; and a mist to arise between myself and His Majesty. In addition to these sensations, I felt extremely unwell. I refer these unpleasant effects, either to the paste with which the posters were affixed to the van: which may have contained some small portion of arsenic; or, to the printer's ink, which may have contained some equally deleterious ingredient. Of this, I cannot be sure. I am only sure that I was not affected, either by the smoke, or the rum- and-water. I was assisted out of the vehicle, in a state of mind which I have only experienced in two other places - I allude to the Pier at Dover, and to the corresponding portion of the town of Calais - and sat upon a door-step until I recovered. The procession had then disappeared. I have since looked anxiously for the King in several other cars, but I have not yet had the happiness of seeing His Majesty.

The Streets - Night]

But the streets of London, to be beheld in the very height of their glory, should be seen on a dark, dull, murky winter's night, when there is just enough damp gently stealing down to make the pavement greasy, without cleansing it of any of its impurities; and when the heavy lazy mist, which hangs over every object, makes the gas-lamps look brighter, and the brilliantly-lighted shops more splendid, from the contrast they present to the darkness around. All the people who are at home on such a night as this, seem disposed to make themselves as snug and comfortable as possible; and the passengers in the streets have excellent reason to envy the fortunate individuals who are seated by their own firesides.

In the larger and better kind of streets, dining parlour curtains are closely drawn, kitchen fires blaze brightly up, and savoury steams of hot dinners salute the nostrils of the hungry wayfarer, as he plods wearily by the area railings. In the suburbs, the muffin boy rings his way down the little street, much more slowly than he is wont to do; for Mrs. Macklin, of No. 4, has no sooner opened her little street-door, and screamed out 'Muffins!' with all her might, than Mrs. Walker, at No. 5, puts her head out of the parlour-window, and screams 'Muffins!' too; and Mrs. Walker has scarcely got the words out of her lips, than Mrs. Peplow, over the way, lets loose Master Peplow, who darts down the street, with a velocity which nothing but buttered muffins in perspective could possibly inspire, and drags the boy back by main force, whereupon Mrs. Macklin and Mrs. Walker, just to save the boy trouble, and to say a few neighbourly words to Mrs. Peplow at the same time, run over the way and buy their muffins at Mrs. Peplow's door, when it appears from the voluntary statement of Mrs. Walker, that her 'kittle's jist a-biling, and the cups and sarsers ready laid,' and that, as it was such a wretched night out o' doors, she'd made up her mind to have a nice, hot, comfortable cup o' tea, a determination at which, by the most singular coincidence, the other two ladies had simultaneously arrived.

After a little conversation about the wretchedness of the weather and the merits of tea, with a digression relative to the viciousness of boys as a rule, and the amiability of Master Peplow as an exception, Mrs. Walker sees her husband coming down the street; and as he must want his tea, poor man, after his dirty walk from the Docks, she instantly runs across, muffins in hand, and Mrs. Macklin does the same, and after a few words to Mrs. Walker, they all pop into their little houses, and slam their little street-doors, which are not opened again for the remainder of the evening, except to the nine o'clock 'beer,' who comes round with a lantern in front of his tray, and says, as he lends Mrs. Walker 'Yesterday's 'Tiser,' that he's blessed if he can hardly hold the pot, much less feel the paper, for it's one of the bitterest nights he ever felt, 'cept the night when the man was frozen to death in the Brick-field.

After a little prophetic conversation with the policeman at the street-corner, touching a probable change in the weather, and the setting-in of a hard frost, the nine o'clock beer returns to his master's house, and employs himself for the remainder of the evening, in assiduously stirring the tap-room fire, and deferentially taking part in the conversation of the worthies assembled round it.

The streets in the vicinity of the Marsh-gate and Victoria Theatre present an appearance of dirt and discomfort on such a night, which the groups who lounge about them in no degree tend to diminish. Even the little block-tin temple sacred to baked potatoes, surmounted by a splendid design in variegated lamps, looks less gay than usual, and as to the kidney-pie stand, its glory has quite departed. The candle in the transparent lamp, manufactured of oil- paper, embellished with 'characters,' has been blown out fifty times, so the kidney-pie merchant, tired with running backwards and forwards to the next wine-vaults, to get a light, has given up the idea of illumination in despair, and the only signs of his 'whereabout,' are the bright sparks, of which a long irregular train is whirled down the street every time he opens his portable oven to hand a hot kidney-pie to a customer.

Flat-fish, oyster, and fruit vendors linger hopelessly in the kennel, in vain endeavouring to attract customers; and the ragged boys who usually disport themselves about the streets, stand crouched in little knots in some projecting doorway, or under the canvas blind of a cheesemonger's, where great flaring gas-lights, unshaded by any glass, display huge piles of blight red and pale yellow cheeses, mingled with little fivepenny dabs of dingy bacon, various tubs of weekly Dorset, and cloudy rolls of 'best fresh.'

Here they amuse themselves with theatrical converse, arising out of their last half-price visit to the Victoria gallery, admire the terrific combat, which is nightly encored, and expatiate on the inimitable manner in which Bill Thompson can 'come the double monkey,' or go through the mysterious involutions of a sailor's hornpipe.

It is nearly eleven o'clock, and the cold thin rain which has been drizzling so long, is beginning to pour down in good earnest; the baked-potato man has departed, the kidney-pie man has just walked away with his warehouse on his arm, the cheesemonger has drawn in his blind, and the boys have dispersed. The constant clicking of pattens on the slippy and uneven pavement, and the rustling of umbrellas, as the wind blows against the shop-windows, bear testimony to the inclemency of the night; and the policeman, with his oilskin cape buttoned closely round him, seems as he holds his hat on his head, and turns round to avoid the gust of wind and rain which drives against him at the street-corner, to be very far from congratulating himself on the prospect before him.

The little chandler's shop with the cracked bell behind the door, whose melancholy tinkling has been regulated by the demand for quarterns of sugar and half-ounces of coffee, is shutting up. The crowds which have been passing to and fro during the whole day, are rapidly dwindling away; and the noise of shouting and quarrelling which issues from the public-houses, is almost the only sound that breaks the melancholy stillness of the night.

There was another, but it has ceased. That wretched woman with the infant in her arms, round whose meagre form the remnant of her own scanty shawl is carefully wrapped, has been attempting to sing some popular ballad, in the hope of wringing a few pence from the compassionate passer-by. A brutal laugh at her weak voice is all she has gained. The tears fall thick and fast down her own pale face; the child is cold and hungry, and its low half-stifled wailing adds to the misery of its wretched mother, as she moans aloud, and sinks despairingly down, on a cold damp door-step.

Singing! How few of those who pass such a miserable creature as this, think of the anguish of heart, the sinking of soul and spirit, which the very effort of singing produces. Bitter mockery! Disease, neglect, and starvation, faintly articulating the words of the joyous ditty, that has enlivened your hours of feasting and merriment, God knows how often! It is no subject of jeering. The weak tremulous voice tells a fearful tale of want and famishing; and the feeble singer of this roaring song may turn away, only to die of cold and hunger.

One o'clock! Parties returning from the different theatres foot it through the muddy streets; cabs, hackney-coaches, carriages, and theatre omnibuses, roll swiftly by; watermen with dim dirty lanterns in their hands, and large brass plates upon their breasts, who have been shouting and rushing about for the last two hours, retire to their watering-houses, to solace themselves with the creature comforts of pipes and purl; the half-price pit and box frequenters of the theatres throng to the different houses of refreshment; and chops, kidneys, rabbits, oysters, stout, cigars, and 'goes' innumerable, are served up amidst a noise and confusion of smoking, running, knife-clattering, and waiter-chattering, perfectly indescribable.

The more musical portion of the play-going community betake themselves to some harmonic meeting. As a matter of curiosity let us follow them thither for a few moments.

In a lofty room of spacious dimensions, are seated some eighty or a hundred guests knocking little pewter measures on the tables, and hammering away, with the handles of their knives, as if they were so many trunk-makers. They are applauding a glee, which has just been executed by the three 'professional gentlemen' at the top of the centre table, one of whom is in the chair, the little pompous man with the bald head just emerging from the collar of his green coat. The others are seated on either side of him, the stout man with the small voice, and the thin-faced dark man in black. The little man in the chair is a most amusing personage, such condescending grandeur, and SUCH a voice!

'Bass!' as the young gentleman near us with the blue stock forcibly remarks to his companion, 'bass! I b'lieve you; he can go down lower than any man: so low sometimes that you can't hear him.' And so he does. To hear him growling away, gradually lower and lower down, till he can't get back again, is the most delightful thing in the world, and it is quite impossible to witness unmoved the impressive solemnity with which he pours forth his soul in 'My 'art's in the 'ighlands,' or 'The brave old Hoak.' The stout man is also addicted to sentimentality, and warbles 'Fly, fly from the world, my Bessy, with me,' or some such song, with lady-like sweetness, and in the most seductive tones imaginable.

'Pray give your orders, gen'l'm'n, pray give your orders,' says the pale-faced man with the red head; and demands for 'goes' of gin and 'goes' of brandy, and pints of stout, and cigars of peculiar mildness, are vociferously made from all parts of the room. The 'professional gentlemen' are in the very height of their glory, and bestow condescending nods, or even a word or two of recognition, on the better-known frequenters of the room, in the most bland and patronising manner possible.

The little round-faced man, with the small brown surtout, white stockings and shoes, is in the comic line; the mixed air of self- denial, and mental consciousness of his own powers, with which he acknowledges the call of the chair, is particularly gratifying. 'Gen'l'men,' says the little pompous man, accompanying the word with a knock of the president's hammer on the table, 'Gen'l'men, allow me to claim your attention, our friend, Mr. Smuggins, will oblige.' - 'Bravo!' shout the company; and Smuggins, after a considerable quantity of coughing by way of symphony, and a most facetious sniff or two, which afford general delight, sings a comic song, with a fal-de-ral, tol-de-ral chorus at the end of every verse, much longer than the verse itself. It is received with unbounded applause, and after some aspiring genius has volunteered a recitation, and failed dismally therein, the little pompous man gives another knock, and says 'Gen'l'men, we will attempt a glee, if you please.' This announcement calls forth tumultuous applause, and the more energetic spirits express the unqualified approbation it affords them, by knocking one or two stout glasses off their legs, a humorous device; but one which frequently occasions some slight altercation when the form of paying the damage is proposed to be gone through by the waiter.

Scenes like these are continued until three or four o'clock in the morning; and even when they close, fresh ones open to the inquisitive novice. But as a description of all of them, however slight, would require a volume, the contents of which, however instructive, would be by no means pleasing, we make our bow, and drop the curtain.

The Child's Story

Once upon a time, a good many years ago, there was a traveller, and he set out upon a journey. It was a magic journey, and was to seem very long when he began it, and very short when he got half way through.

He travelled along a rather dark path for some little time, without meeting anything, until at last he came to a beautiful child. So he said to the child, "What do you do here?" And the child said, "I am always at play. Come and play with me!"

So, he played with that child, the whole day long, and they were very merry. The sky was so blue, the sun was so bright, the water was so sparkling, the leaves were so green, the flowers were so lovely, and they heard such singing-birds and saw so many butteries, that everything was beautiful. This was in fine weather. When it rained, they loved to watch the falling drops, and to smell the fresh scents. When it blew, it was delightful to listen to the wind, and fancy what it said, as it came rushing from its home, where was that, they wondered! whistling and howling, driving the clouds before it, bending the trees, rumbling in the chimneys, shaking the house, and making the sea roar in fury. But, when it snowed, that was best of all; for, they liked nothing so well as to look up at the white flakes falling fast and thick, like down from the breasts of millions of white birds; and to see how smooth and deep the drift was; and to listen to the hush upon the paths and roads.

They had plenty of the finest toys in the world, and the most astonishing picture-books: all about scimitars and slippers and turbans, and dwarfs and giants and genii and fairies, and blue- beards and bean-stalks and riches and caverns and forests and Valentines and Orsons: and all new and all true.

But, one day, of a sudden, the traveller lost the child. He called to him over and over again, but got no answer. So, he went upon his road, and went on for a little while without meeting anything, until at last he came to a handsome boy. So, he said to the boy, "What do you do here?" And the boy said, "I am always learning. Come and learn with me."

So he learned with that boy about Jupiter and Juno, and the Greeks and the Romans, and I don't know what, and learned more than I could tell, or he either, for he soon forgot a great deal of it. But, they were not always learning; they had the merriest games that ever were played. They rowed upon the river in summer, and skated on the ice in winter; they were active afoot, and active on horseback; at cricket, and all games at ball; at prisoner's base, hare and hounds, follow my leader, and more sports than I can think of; nobody could beat them. They had holidays too, and Twelfth cakes, and parties where they danced till midnight, and real Theatres where they saw palaces of real gold and silver rise out of the real earth, and saw all the wonders of the world at once. As to friends, they had such dear friends and so many of them, that I want the time to reckon them up. They were all young, like the handsome boy, and were never to be strange to one another all their lives through.

Still, one day, in the midst of all these pleasures, the traveller lost the boy as he had lost the child, and, after calling to him in vain, went on upon his journey. So he went on for a little while without seeing anything, until at last he came to a young man. So, he said to the young man, "What do you do here?" And the young man said, "I am always in love. Come and love with me."

So, he went away with that young man, and presently they came to one of the prettiest girls that ever was seen, just like Fanny in the corner there, and she had eyes like Fanny, and hair like Fanny, and dimples like Fanny's, and she laughed and coloured just as Fanny does while I am talking about her. So, the young man fell in love directly, just as Somebody I won't mention, the first time he came here, did with Fanny. Well! he was teased sometimes, just as Somebody used to be by Fanny; and they quarrelled sometimes, just as Somebody and Fanny used to quarrel; and they made it up, and sat in the dark, and wrote letters every day, and never were happy asunder, and were always looking out for one another and pretending not to, and were engaged at Christmas-time, and sat close to one another by the fire, and were going to be married very soon, all exactly like Somebody I won't mention, and Fanny!

But, the traveller lost them one day, as he had lost the rest of his friends, and, after calling to them to come back, which they never did, went on upon his journey. So, he went on for a little while without seeing anything, until at last he came to a middle-aged gentleman. So, he said to the gentleman, "What are you doing here?" And his answer was, "I am always busy. Come and be busy with me!"

So, he began to be very busy with that gentleman, and they went on through the wood together. The whole journey was through a wood, only it had been open and green at first, like a wood in spring; and now began to be thick and dark, like a wood in summer; some of the little trees that had come out earliest, were even turning brown. The gentleman was not alone, but had a lady of about the same age with him, who was his Wife; and they had children, who were with them too. So, they all went on together through the wood, cutting down the trees, and making a path through the branches and the fallen leaves, and carrying burdens, and working hard.

Sometimes, they came to a long green avenue that opened into deeper woods. Then they would hear a very little, distant voice crying, "Father, father, I am another child! Stop for me!" And presently they would see a very little figure, growing larger as it came along, running to join them. When it came up, they all crowded round it, and kissed and welcomed it; and then they all went on together.

Sometimes, they came to several avenues at once, and then they all stood still, and one of the children said, "Father, I am going to sea," and another said, "Father, I am going to India," and another, "Father, I am going to seek my fortune where I can," and another, "Father, I am going to Heaven!" So, with many tears at parting, they went, solitary, down those avenues, each child upon its way; and the child who went to Heaven, rose into the golden air and vanished.

Whenever these partings happened, the traveller looked at the gentleman, and saw him glance up at the sky above the trees, where the day was beginning to decline, and the sunset to come on. He saw, too, that his hair was turning grey. But, they never could rest long, for they had their journey to perform, and it was necessary for them to be always busy.

At last, there had been so many partings that there were no children left, and only the traveller, the gentleman, and the lady, went upon their way in company. And now the wood was yellow; and now brown; and the leaves, even of the forest trees, began to fall.

So, they came to an avenue that was darker than the rest, and were pressing forward on their journey without looking down it when the lady stopped.

"My husband," said the lady. "I am called."

They listened, and they heard a voice a long way down the avenue, say, "Mother, mother!"

It was the voice of the first child who had said, "I am going to Heaven!" and the father said, "I pray not yet. The sunset is very near. I pray not yet!"

But, the voice cried, "Mother, mother!" without minding him, though his hair was now quite white, and tears were on his face.

Then, the mother, who was already drawn into the shade of the dark avenue and moving away with her arms still round his neck, kissed him, and said, "My dearest, I am summoned, and I go!" And she was gone. And the traveller and he were left alone together.

And they went on and on together, until they came to very near the end of the wood: so near, that they could see the sunset shining red before them through the trees.

Yet, once more, while he broke his way among the branches, the traveller lost his friend. He called and called, but there was no reply, and when he passed out of the wood, and saw the peaceful sun going down upon a wide purple prospect, he came to an old man sitting on a fallen tree. So, he said to the old man, "What do you do here?" And the old man said with a calm smile, "I am always remembering. Come and remember with me!"

So the traveller sat down by the side of that old man, face to face with the serene sunset; and all his friends came softly back and stood around him. The beautiful child, the handsome boy, the young man in love, the father, mother, and children:

every one of them was there, and he had lost nothing. So, he loved them all, and was kind and forbearing with them all, and was always pleased to watch them all, and they all honoured and loved him. And I think the traveller must be yourself, dear Grandfather, because this what you do to us, and what we do to you.

The Poor Relation's Story

He was very reluctant to take precedence of so many respected members of the family, by beginning the round of stories they were to relate as they sat in a goodly circle by the Christmas fire; and he modestly suggested that it would be more correct if "John our esteemed host" (whose health he begged to drink) would have the kindness to begin. For as to himself, he said, he was so little used to lead the way that really. But as they all cried out here, that he must begin, and agreed with one voice that he might, could, would, and should begin, he left off rubbing his hands, and took his legs out from under his armchair, and did begin.

I have no doubt (said the poor relation) that I shall surprise the assembled members of our family, and particularly John our esteemed host to whom we are so much indebted for the great hospitality with which he has this day entertained us, by the confession I am going to make. But, if you do me the honour to be surprised at anything that falls from a person so unimportant in the family as I am, I can only say that I shall be scrupulously accurate in all I relate.

I am not what I am supposed to be. I am quite another thing. Perhaps before I go further, I had better glance at what I AM supposed to be.

It is supposed, unless I mistake, the assembled members of our family will correct me if I do, which is very likely (here the poor relation looked mildly about him for contradiction); that I am nobody's enemy but my own. That I never met with any particular success in anything. That I failed in business because I was unbusiness-like and credulous in not being prepared for the interested designs of my partner. That I failed in love, because I was ridiculously trustful in thinking it impossible that Christiana could deceive me. That I failed in my expectations from my uncle Chill, on account of not being as sharp as he could have wished in worldly matters. That, through life, I have been rather put upon and disappointed in a general way. That I am at present a bachelor of between fifty-nine and sixty years of age, living on a limited income in the form of a quarterly allowance, to which I see that John our esteemed host wishes me to make no further allusion.

The supposition as to my present pursuits and habits is to the following effect.

I live in a lodging in the Clapham Road, a very clean back room, in a very respectable house, where I am expected not to be at home in the day-time, unless poorly; and which I usually leave in the morning at nine o'clock, on pretence of going to business. I take my breakfast, my roll and butter, and my half-pint of coffee, at the old-established coffee-shop near Westminster Bridge; and then I go into the City, I don't know why, and sit in Garraway's Coffee House, and on 'Change, and walk about, and look into a few offices and counting-houses where some of my relations or acquaintance are so good as to tolerate me, and where I stand by the fire if the weather happens to be cold. I get through the day in this way until five o'clock, and then I dine: at a cost, on the average, of one and threepence. Having still a little money to spend on my evening's entertainment, I look into the old-established coffee-shop as I go home, and take my cup of tea, and perhaps my bit of toast. So, as the large hand of the clock makes its way round to the morning hour again, I make my way round to the Clapham Road again, and go to bed when I get to my lodging, fire being expensive, and being objected to by the family on account of its giving trouble and making a dirt.

Sometimes, one of my relations or acquaintances is so obliging as to ask me to dinner. Those are holiday occasions, and then I generally walk in the Park. I am a solitary man, and seldom walk with anybody. Not that I am avoided because I am shabby; for I am not at all shabby, having always a very good suit of black on (or rather Oxford mixture, which has the appearance of black and wears much better); but I have got into a habit of speaking low, and being rather silent, and my spirits are not high, and I am sensible that I am not an attractive companion.

The only exception to this general rule is the child of my first cousin, Little Frank. I have a particular affection for that child, and he takes very kindly to me. He is a diffident boy by nature; and in a crowd he is soon run over, as I may say, and forgotten. He and I, however, get on exceedingly well. I have a fancy that the poor child will in time succeed to my peculiar position in the family. We talk but little; still, we understand each other. We walk about, hand in hand; and without much speaking he knows what I mean, and I know what he means. When he was very little indeed, I used to take him to the windows of the toy-shops, and show him the toys inside. It is surprising how soon he found out that I would have made him a great many presents if I had been in circumstances to do it.

Little Frank and I go and look at the outside of the Monument, he is very fond of the Monument, and at the Bridges, and at all the sights that are free. On two of my birthdays, we have dined on e-la-mode beef, and gone at half-price to the play, and been deeply interested. I was once walking with him in Lombard Street, which we often visit on account of my having mentioned to him that there are great riches there, he is very fond of Lombard Street, when a gentleman said to me as he passed by, "Sir, your little son has dropped his glove." I assure you, if you will excuse my remarking on so trivial a circumstance, this accidental mention of the child as mine, quite touched my heart and brought the foolish tears into my eyes.

When Little Frank is sent to school in the country, I shall be very much at a loss what to do with myself, but I have the intention of walking down there once a month and seeing him on a half holiday. I am told he will then be at play upon the Heath; and if my visits should be objected to, as unsettling the child, I can see him from a distance without his seeing me, and walk back again. His mother comes of a highly genteel family, and rather disapproves, I am aware, of our being too much together. I know that I am not calculated to improve his retiring disposition; but I think he would miss me beyond the feeling of the moment if we were wholly separated.

When I die in the Clapham Road, I shall not leave much more in this world than I shall take out of it; but, I happen to have a miniature of a bright-faced boy, with a curling head, and an open shirt-frill waving down his bosom (my mother had it taken for me, but I can't believe that it was ever like), which will be worth nothing to sell, and which I shall beg may he given to Frank. I have written my dear boy a little letter with it, in which I have told him that I felt very sorry to part from him, though bound to confess that I knew no reason why I should remain here. I have given him some short advice, the best in my power, to take warning of the consequences of being nobody's enemy but his own; and I have endeavoured to comfort him for what I fear he will consider a bereavement, by pointing out to him, that I was only a superfluous something to every one but him; and that having by some means failed to find a place in this great assembly, I am better out of it.

Such (said the poor relation, clearing his throat and beginning to speak a little louder) is the general impression about me. Now, it is a remarkable circumstance which forms the aim and purpose of my story, that this is all wrong. This is not my life, and these are not my habits. I do not even live in the Clapham Road. Comparatively speaking, I am very seldom there. I reside, mostly, in a, I am almost ashamed to say the word, it sounds so full of pretension, in a Castle. I do not mean that it is an old baronial habitation, but still it is a building always known to every one by the name of a Castle. In it, I preserve the particulars of my history; they run thus:

It was when I first took John Spatter (who had been my clerk) into partnership, and when I was still a young man of not more than five- and-twenty, residing in the house of my uncle Chill, from whom I had considerable expectations, that I ventured to propose to Christiana. I had loved Christiana a long time. She was very beautiful, and very winning in all respects. I rather mistrusted her widowed mother, who I feared was of a plotting and mercenary turn of mind; but, I thought as well of her as I could, for Christiana's sake. I never had loved any one but Christiana, and she had been all the world, and O far more than all the world, to me, from our childhood!

Christiana accepted me with her mother's consent, and I was rendered very happy indeed. My life at my uncle Chill's was of a spare dull kind, and my garret chamber was as dull, and bare, and cold, as an upper prison room in some stern northern fortress. But, having Christiana's love, I wanted nothing upon earth. I would not have changed my lot with any human being.

Avarice was, unhappily, my uncle Chill's master-vice. Though he was rich, he pinched, and scraped, and clutched, and lived miserably. As Christiana had no fortune, I was for some time a little fearful of confessing our engagement to him; but, at length I wrote him a letter, saying how it all truly was. I put it into his hand one night, on going to bed.

As I came down-stairs next morning, shivering in the cold December air; colder in my uncle's unwarmed house than in the street, where the winter sun did sometimes shine, and which was at all events enlivened by cheerful faces and voices passing along; I carried a heavy heart towards the long, low breakfast-room in which my uncle sat. It was a large room with a small fire, and there was a great bay window in it which the rain had marked in the night as if with the tears of houseless people. It stared upon a raw yard, with a cracked stone pavement, and some rusted iron railings half uprooted, whence an ugly out-building that had once been a dissecting-room (in the time of the great surgeon who had mortgaged the house to my uncle), stared at it.

We rose so early always, that at that time of the year we breakfasted by candle-light. When I went into the room, my uncle was so contracted by the cold, and so huddled together in his chair behind the one dim candle, that I did not see him until I was close to the table.

As I held out my hand to him, he caught up his stick (being infirm, he always walked about the house with a stick), and made a blow at me, and said, "You fool!"

"Uncle," I returned, "I didn't expect you to be so angry as this." Nor had I expected it, though he was a hard and angry old man.

"You didn't expect!" said he; "when did you ever expect? When did you ever calculate, or look forward, you contemptible dog?"

"These are hard words, uncle!"

"Hard words? Feathers, to pelt such an idiot as you with," said he. "Here! Betsy Snap! Look at him!"

Betsy Snap was a withered, hard-favoured, yellow old woman, our only domestic, always employed, at this time of the morning, in rubbing my uncle's legs. As my uncle adjured her to look at me, he put his lean grip on the crown of her head, she kneeling beside him, and turned her face towards me. An involuntary thought connecting them both with the Dissecting Room, as it must often have been in the surgeon's time, passed across my mind in the midst of my anxiety.

"Look at the snivelling milksop!" said my uncle. "Look at the baby! This is the gentleman who, people say, is nobody's enemy but his own. This is the gentleman who can't say no. This is the gentleman who was making such large profits in his business that he must needs take a partner, t'other day. This is the gentleman who is going to marry a wife without a penny, and who falls into the hands of Jezabels who are speculating on my death!"

I knew, now, how great my uncle's rage was; for nothing short of his being almost beside himself would have induced him to utter that concluding word, which he held in such repugnance that it was never spoken or hinted at before him on any account.

"On my death," he repeated, as if he were defying me by defying his own abhorrence of the word. "On my death, death, Death! But I'll spoil the speculation. Eat your last under this roof, you feeble wretch, and may it choke you!"

You may suppose that I had not much appetite for the breakfast to which I was bidden in these terms; but, I took my accustomed seat. I saw that I was repudiated henceforth by my uncle; still I could bear that very well, possessing Christiana's heart.

He emptied his basin of bread and milk as usual, only that he took it on his knees with his chair turned away from the table where I sat. When he had done, he carefully snuffed out the candle; and the cold, slate-coloured, miserable day looked in upon us.

"Now, Mr. Michael," said he, "before we part, I should like to have a word with these ladies in your presence."

"As you will, sir," I returned; "but you deceive yourself, and wrong us, cruelly, if you suppose that there is any feeling at stake in this contract but pure, disinterested, faithful love."

To this, he only replied, "You lie!" and not one other word.

We went, through half-thawed snow and half-frozen rain, to the house where Christiana and her mother lived. My uncle knew them very well. They were sitting at their breakfast, and were surprised to see us at that hour.

"Your servant, ma'am," said my uncle to the mother. "You divine the purpose of my visit, I dare say, ma'am. I understand there is a world of pure, disinterested, faithful love cooped up here. I am happy to bring it all it wants, to make it complete. I bring you your son-in-law, ma'am, and you, your husband, miss. The gentleman is a perfect stranger to me, but I wish him joy of his wise bargain."

He snarled at me as he went out, and I never saw him again.

It is altogether a mistake (continued the poor relation) to suppose that my dear Christiana, over-persuaded and influenced by her mother, married a rich man, the dirt from whose carriage wheels is often, in these changed times, thrown upon me as she rides by. No, no. She married me.

The way we came to be married rather sooner than we intended, was this. I took a frugal lodging and was saving and planning for her sake, when, one day, she spoke to me with great earnestness, and said:

"My dear Michael, I have given you my heart. I have said that I loved you, and I have pledged myself to be your wife. I am as much yours through all changes of good and evil as if we had been married on the day when such words passed between us. I know you well, and know that if we should be separated and our union broken off, your whole life would be shadowed, and all that might, even now, be stronger in your character for the conflict with the world would then be weakened to the shadow of what it is!"

"God help me, Christiana!" said I. "You speak the truth."

"Michael!" said she, putting her hand in mine, in all maidenly devotion, "let us keep apart no longer. It is but for me to say that I can live contented upon such means as you have, and I well know you are happy. I say so from my heart. Strive no more alone; let us strive together. My dear Michael, it is not right that I should keep secret from you what you do not suspect, but what distresses my whole life. My mother: without considering that what you have lost, you have lost for me, and on the assurance of my faith: sets her heart on riches, and urges another suit upon me, to my misery. I cannot bear this, for to bear it is to be untrue to you. I would rather share your struggles than look on. I want no better home than you can give me. I know that you will aspire and labour with a higher courage if I am wholly yours, and let it be so when you will!"

I was blest indeed, that day, and a new world opened to me. We were married in a very little while, and I took my wife to our happy home. That was the beginning of the residence I have spoken of; the Castle we have ever since inhabited together, dates from that time. All our children have been born in it. Our first child, now married, was a little girl, whom we called Christiana. Her son is so like Little Frank, that I hardly know which is which.

The current impression as to my partner's dealings with me is also quite erroneous. He did not begin to treat me coldly, as a poor simpleton, when my uncle and I so fatally quarrelled; nor did he afterwards gradually possess himself of our business and edge me out. On the contrary, he behaved to me with the utmost good faith and honour.

Matters between us took this turn:- On the day of my separation from my uncle, and even before the arrival at our counting-house of my trunks (which he sent after me, NOT carriage paid), I went down to our room of business, on our little wharf, overlooking the river; and there I told John Spatter what had happened. John did not say, in reply, that rich old relatives were palpable facts, and that love and sentiment were moonshine and fiction. He addressed me thus:

"Michael," said John, "we were at school together, and I generally had the knack of getting on better than you, and making a higher reputation."

"You had, John," I returned.

"Although" said John, "I borrowed your books and lost them; borrowed your pocket-money, and never repaid it; got you to buy my damaged knives at a higher price than I had given for them new; and to own to the windows that I had broken."

"All not worth mentioning, John Spatter," said I, "but certainly true."

"When you were first established in this infant business, which promises to thrive so well," pursued John, "I came to you, in my search for almost any employment, and you made me your clerk."

"Still not worth mentioning, my dear John Spatter," said I; "still, equally true."

"And finding that I had a good head for business, and that I was really useful TO the business, you did not like to retain me in that capacity, and thought it an act of justice soon to make me your partner."

"Still less worth mentioning than any of those other little circumstances you have recalled, John Spatter," said I; "for I was, and am, sensible of your merits and my deficiencies."

"Now, my good friend," said John, drawing my arm through his, as he had had a habit of doing at school; while two vessels outside the windows of our counting-house, which were shaped like the stern windows of a ship, went lightly down the river with the tide, as John and I might then be sailing away in company, and in trust and confidence, on our voyage of life; "let there, under these friendly circumstances, be a right understanding between us. You are too easy, Michael. You are nobody's enemy but your own. If I were to give you that damaging character among our connexion, with a shrug, and a shake of the head, and a sigh; and if I were further to abuse the trust you place in me"

"But you never will abuse it at all, John," I observed.

"Never!" said he; "but I am putting a case, I say, and if I were further to abuse that trust by keeping this piece of our common affairs in the dark, and this other piece in the light, and again this other piece in the twilight, and so on, I should strengthen my strength, and weaken your weakness, day by day, until at last I found myself on the high road to fortune, and you left behind on some bare common, a hopeless number of miles out of the way."

"Exactly so," said I.

"To prevent this, Michael," said John Spatter, "or the remotest chance of this, there must be perfect openness between us. Nothing must be concealed, and we must have but one interest."

"My dear John Spatter," I assured him, "that is precisely what I mean."

"And when you are too easy," pursued John, his face glowing with friendship, "you must allow me to prevent that imperfection in your nature from being taken advantage of, by any one; you must not expect me to humour it"

"My dear John Spatter," I interrupted, "I DON'T expect you to humour it. I want to correct it."

"And I, too," said John.

"Exactly so!" cried I. "We both have the same end in view; and, honourably seeking it, and fully trusting one another, and having but one interest, ours will be a prosperous and happy partnership."

"I am sure of it!" returned John Spatter. And we shook hands most affectionately.

I took John home to my Castle, and we had a very happy day. Our partnership throve well. My friend and partner supplied what I wanted, as I had foreseen that he would, and by improving both the business and myself, amply acknowledged any little rise in life to which I had helped him.

I am not (said the poor relation, looking at the fire as he slowly rubbed his hands) very rich, for I never cared to be that; but I have enough, and am above all moderate wants and anxieties. My Castle is not a splendid place, but it is very comfortable, and it has a warm and cheerful air, and is quite a picture of Home.

Our eldest girl, who is very like her mother, married John Spatter's eldest son. Our two families are closely united in other ties of attachment. It is very pleasant of an evening, when we are all assembled together, which frequently happens, and when John and I talk over old times, and the one interest there has always been between us.

I really do not know, in my Castle, what loneliness is. Some of our children or grandchildren are always about it, and the young voices of my descendants are delightful, O, how delightful! to me to hear. My dearest and most devoted wife, ever faithful, ever loving, ever helpful and sustaining and consoling, is the priceless blessing of my house; from whom all its other blessings spring. We are rather a musical family, and when Christiana sees me, at any time, a little weary or depressed, she steals to the piano and sings a gentle air she used to sing when we were first betrothed. So weak a man am I, that I cannot bear to hear it from any other source. They played it once, at the Theatre, when I was there with Little Frank; and the child said wondering, "Cousin Michael, whose hot tears are these that have fallen on my hand!"

Such is my Castle, and such are the real particulars of my life therein preserved. I often take Little Frank home there. He is very welcome to my grandchildren, and they play together. At this time of the year, the Christmas and New Year time, I am seldom out of my Castle. For, the associations of the season seem to hold me there, and the precepts of the season seem to teach me that it is well to be there.

"And the Castle is" observed a grave, kind voice among the company.

"Yes. My Castle," said the poor relation, shaking his head as he still looked at the fire, "is in the Air. John our esteemed host suggests its situation accurately. My Castle is in the Air! I have done. Will you be so good as to pass the story?"

Charles Dickens - A Short Biography

Charles Dickens (1812-1870) is regarded by many readers and literary critics to be THE major English novelist of the Victorian Age. He is remembered today as the author of a series of weighty novels which have been translated into many languages and promoted to the rank of World Classics. The latter include, but are not limited to, *The Adventures of Oliver Twist*, *A Tale of Two Cities*, *David Copperfield*, *A Christmas Carol*, *Hard Times*, *Great Expectations* and *The Old Curiosity Shop*.

Birth and Childhood's Hardships

By and large, Charles Dickens's life story is one of somebody who is born and raised in dire straits to become one of the greatest men who have marked human history and thought. It is a perfect example of how the plight of the deprived and the destitute could transform into a precious incentive that pushes them to challenge their circumstances and to unexpectedly excel and shine.

Charles Dickens was born in Portsmouth on February 7th, 1812. His father John Dickens worked as a simple accounting clerk at the Naval Pay Office and the family's pecuniary situation was almost always uneven. When Charles was only two years, the family had to move to London, then later to Chatham. For financial reasons, Charles did not have adequate education. He rather had to leave school at a very young age to work at a polishing and blacking factory. To add insult to injury, Charles's father was imprisoned in 1824 after failing to pay a 40-pound debt.

Charles's experience at the factory played a tremendous role in building the novelist's personality and in deepening his concerns about working children and about the working class in general. Dickens's precocious maturity and the serious responsibilities that he had as a little child left a clear impression on many of his young characters, such as Oliver Twist, David Copperfield and Pip in *Great Expectations*. The hardships that Charles Dickens personally went through made him much interested in defending the poor, in fighting social injustice through exposing its blatant manifestations and in accentuating the importance of having decent work conditions.

Between 1824 and 1827, Dickens's father, who eventually managed to pay his debts, offered Charles the opportunity to attend a private school in North London, the Wellington House Academy. The experience surely enriched the young man's knowledge of the rules of writing and rhetoric and whetted his appetite for 18th-century novels and for the picaresque novels that adorned his father's library. However, during this period, Charles still had to experience another disappointment when his mother refused to spare him the strenuous job at the blacking factory even after the relative improvement of the family's financial situation. The mother's decision had a great psychological impact on young Charles and even influenced his vision of gender roles as he thought that the mother should not be the decision-maker in the family.

Early Publications

Young Charles Dickens occupied numerous jobs and worked hard to learn shorthand. This long and diversified professional experience had a patent impact on his different writings. Indeed, after the blacking factory experience, Dickens first worked as a clerk for attorneys, which allowed him to learn about the legal system and its principles, to become a free-lance reporter for Doctor's Commons Courts in 1829. Later, he even wrote reports for the House of Commons before starting to work for newspapers, magazines and journals.

It was in 1833 that Dickens started writing short stories for a number of literary magazines and journals such as *The Monthly Magazine.* A collection of these texts was later pseudonymously published under the title *Sketches by Boz*. Thanks to Dickens's humor and exceptional writing style, the latter publication was relatively successful, but not as successful as *The Pickwick Papers* whose serial publication sold thousands of copies and raised Dickens to considerable fame. In 1836, he started writing short texts to be published with the humorous illustrations of the famous artist Robert Seymour. These first successes encouraged Dickens to carry on publishing other stories in the form of series. Dickens's next creation was *Oliver Twist* which was published between 1837 and 1839.

It is noteworthy that most of Dickens's novels were published in the form of monthly and weekly chapters which, according to critics and biographers, allowed him to evaluate and adjust his characterizations and plots to meet the expectations of his readership. It was also during this period that Dickens started his long career as a literary magazine editor.

Loves and Marriage

Charles Dickens got married on April 2nd, 1836 to Catherine Thomson Hogarth after one year of engagement. They settled at the famous Furnival's Inn in Holborn, London, before they moved to their home in Bloomsbury. The house was transformed into the Charles Dickens Museum in 1925. Charles and Catherine, who lived there with the first three of their ten children, were joined by Charles's brother Frederick and Catherine's sister Mary. The latter was reported to have had a very special place in Charles's heart. After dying in his own arms in 1837 following a sudden illness, she became a source of inspiration for some of his female characters. After three years of marriage, Dickens's success and rising income made him leave the house for larger and more luxurious estates.

Catherine Hogarth was not Dickens's only love, however. Indeed, biographers report that Dickens's relation with his wife was sandwiched by two other romantic affairs. First, there was Maria Beadnell, a banker's daughter, with whom Dickens fell in love when he was only eighteen years old. The relationship ended three years later when Maria's parents apparently intervened. The other love story that Dickens went through started in 1857 and pushed him to divorce Catherine the following year. It was when Dickens was having a group of young actresses for the staging of his play *The Frozen Deep* that he fell in love with the actress Ellen Ternan who was 27 years younger than him.

Major Achievements

Charles's first success with *The Pickwick Papers* and *Oliver Twist* only pushed him to devote more time and energy to his writing and editorial activities. After publishing *Nicholas Nickleby* between 1838 and 1839, he started a new project in 1840 that he entitled *Master Humphrey's Clock*. The latter is a collection of stories that share the same frame and have recurring characters. It was among this collection that the two major works *The Old Curiosity Shop* and *Barnaby Rudge* were serially published.

After visiting the United States of America in 1842, Dickens developed a rather negative view of the New World which was mainly depicted in his travelogue *American Notes for General Circulation* and also in his picaresque novel *Martin Chuzzlewit*. The latter included very harsh satire of the republic and strongly denounced its institution of slavery. However, the fury that Dickens caused among some American circles was soon quietened with the publication of *A Christmas Carol* in 1843. The book, which is considered by many as the novelist's finest opus, was celebrated both in England and America.

Two other Christmas books followed respectively in 1834 and 1845. They are *The Chimes* and *The Cricket on the Hearth*. During this period, Dickens also published a new travelogue that he entitled *Pictures from Italy* following his stay in the Mediterranean country. Another Christmas story entitled *The Haunted Man* was published in 1848, which was preceded by *Dombey and Son* (1847) and *The Battle of Life* (1847) and followed by David Copperfield (1849-1850), *Bleak House* (1852-1853) and *Hard Times* (1854).

It was in 1853 that Dickens started organizing public performances in which he presented his literary works. By this time, he also started to collaborate with Wilkie Collins on a number of short stories and plays. *Little Dorrit* started as a monthly serial in 1855 to be finished in 1857. Later, two of Dickens's most valuable works were published: *A Tale of Two Cities* (1859) and *Great Expectations* (1861). They were both published in the weekly periodical, *All the Year Round*, which he founded and edited himself.

Apart from his writings, Dickens's main profitable activity was the public reading of his novels. Along with the money he earned thanks to his successful publications, public readings allowed Dickens to buy his dream house (Gad's Hill Place, Kent), to offer financial help to his parents and brothers and to engage in charitable activities.

Twilight and Death

During the 1860s, Dickens carried on organizing more reading tours. In addition to the many events he had in England, he visited France, the United States, Scotland and Ireland on many an occasion. In 1864, he started his last complete novel, *Our Mutual Friend*. However, by 1865, his health started to waver. This was mainly because of the physical and intellectual exhaustion to which he subjected himself. Furthermore, Dickens was psychologically traumatized in 1865 following a train crash. He was with his beloved Ellen Ternan on their way back from Paris when their train derailed to cause a big number of casualties. Although Dickens was able to collect his courage and managed to help the wounded and comfort them, the picture of the disaster affected him greatly and could never be erased from his mind.

For health reasons, Dickens cancelled many of his programmed readings between 1868 and 1870. On April 22nd, 1869, he had a stroke. The latter was followed by a second stroke on June 8th, 1870, while he was working on his novel *The Mystery of Edwin Drood* which would remain unfinished. The next day, he passed away. Charles Dickens today rests in The Poets' Corner of Westminster Abbey.

www.ingramcontent.com/pod-product-compliance
Lightning Source LLC
Chambersburg PA
CBHW061456170626
46811CB00004B/1539